LOOSE CANN

Meet the Lord Chamberlain's Men:

Chris (Skip) Hastings: He leads this secret gang and is its chief protagonist. The rest of the gang have supported him in his rage against hypocrisy for decades. He is currently living, and expected to die soon, in Malta.

Ricky (Scalesy) Sharpe: A wealthy plumber who has a successful business and some global connections. Not to be underestimated but frequently is. Totally loyal to Chris and aware of those that aren't.

Trude Shaw: Is the only female, founder member of the gang. Trude has a heart of gold but is not to be trifled with. Her secret, from the other 'Men', is that she has never been asked to support any of Chris's projects.

Steve (Pup) Richardson: He is by far the youngest of the group and is the son of the late Lord Chamberlain's Men' co-founder Geoff. He lusts after ex-tennis professional and socialite Charlene (Charlie) Wright. Pup is a reformed alcoholic and is now making his name as a corporate events' magician.

Matt (Tricks) Robinson: He is a gym co-owner, drugs dealer and look alike for a world wrestling hall of famer. He owes Chris his freedom but isn't taking kindly to Dave giving him orders.

Steph Holding: This senior civil servant is a recent lover of Chris and an honorary member of the Lord Chamberlain's Men. Steph is wracked by her conscience as to how much she wants to know about Chris's activities and how much she should tell her boss.

Dave (Old Dog) Moore: The oldest school friend of Chris. He now has a major role in actioning Chris's plans. He is the joker in the pack at the Lord Chamberlain's Men get-togethers. Dave is dangerous, spiteful and his constant smile hides the guiltiest of secrets.

Nick (Loadsa) Burgess: Spending his time travelling throughout Europe and the USA this slick global executive, of one of the major multi-level marketing companies, is under considerable stress. His role in the Lord Chamberlain's Men is to feed Chris with the location of Chris's targets at any point in time.

LOOSE CANNON

Tony Robinson OBE

All the world's a stage,
And all the men and women merely players;
They have their exits and their entrances,
And one man in his time plays many parts,
His acts being seven ages.

William Shakespeare: 'As You Like It'

First published in Great Britain by The Business Advisory Bureau
Limited October 2017

This paperback and special review limited edition published October
2017

The Business Advisory Bureau Limited
Kirkland
Church End
Milton Bryan
Milton Keynes
MK17 9HU

Paperback ISBN 9781787231849
e-book ISBN 9781787231856

Format by Jo Harrison www.ebook-formatting.co.uk
Cover Design Ryan Ashcroft www.loveyourcovers.com

Thanks To:

Writer, journalist and broadcaster, Amanda Thomas, for helping, at the end of this marathon project, to develop the emotions of the three main female characters.

My brave wife, Eileen, Carl, Alan and Sinead for keeping me going and allowing me to spend a year on the wonderful island of Malta to write this novel.

My business, publishing partner and best friend, Clare Francis, for encouraging me and improving my writing for over thirty years.

Tina Boden, fab co-founder with me of the annual #MicroBizMattersDay who has built our massive informal and campaigning network of networks with the shadow of 'Loose Cannon' always upon her.

Jo Harrison for being the best and most professional VA and friend any writer could hope for and who has formatted all my books and promoted our crazy publishing and enterprising adventures for many years now.

Most of all thank you to my friends and the readers of the many drafts of Loose Cannon that have given me such valuable feedback to improve the content.

My website is TonyRobinsonOBE.com and please follow me on twitter @TonyRobinsonOBE

You can read my poetry, novels and satire on
www.FreedomfromBossesForever.com

What is a 'Review and First Edition'?

Rest assured that you are reading the complete first edition of Loose Cannon. We've found, with previous books, that we increase the readership by publishing real reader reviews. So, we've published this limited first edition to gather reader reviews. If your reviews are positive we may even interest one of the bigger publishers in this novel and/or the next in the series.

Please publish your reviews, giving your full name, if you will allow us to use your review, on Amazon. Goodreads or email to tonyrobinsonobe@gmail.com. Many thanks.

LOOSE CANNON

Contents:

ACT ONE: NOVEMBER 2011

CHAPTER ONE: Smoke and Mirrors

Conspirator: a member of a group of people planning a subversive act

1.

I'M NO JULIAN WIKILEAKS

Fighter jets and military helicopters overhead. An ear-splitting bang. Nobody moves. Applause. Cannon fire - the saluting battery for the tourists.

Chris is seated in the outdoor café at Upper Barrakka Gardens in Valletta. He looks up to check that he is understood. Then he wipes away the words with the side of his hand.

2.

'He's finally flipped, Steph. I hardly recognised him' said Nick, putting his forefinger to his temple to signal insanity.

Steph could see Nick well on Skype. Nick Burgess was in a red and white, minimally furnished, hi tech, executive office at Supramax Life's Chicago HQ. Steph was at the breakfast bar in her kitchen in Sheffield, England with a laptop precariously balanced on a pile of books and magazines that were on top of a stool. She was sitting, cross-legged, on another stool, wearing a russet blouse, grey suit trousers and no shoes. She was eating a slice of toast whilst asking Nick, who she'd never really warmed to, questions about Chris.

Nick had been 'shooting the breeze', as Steph, liked to call it, with her occasional lover, Chris. Nick had recently been in Malta on business and called in to see his old friend. Tomorrow Steph would be seeing more of Chris's oldest friends at the ATP World Tennis Finals at the O2 Arena in London. They would want to know, some hopefully, whether Nick thought Chris was any closer to death's door.

Short open questions would elicit long answers and allow Steph to finish her toast and green tea before she dashed out the door to catch the tram to work. It was just after seven o'clock in the morning, UK time.

'What did he look like then?'

'Just weird, Steph. He looked as if he was in fancy dress or perhaps he's just acting out the batty Englishman. He's always been a drama queen. He was wearing all red, apart from black cargo shorts. Red T shirt, red trainers, red trainer socks, red Skull Candy headphones, red rimmed shades and a red and, wait for this, silk scarf covering his mouth, topped off by a red and black striped trilby-type hat.

The hat looked like something you'd wear in a Ska band. He'd put an 'I love Malta' badge on the hat and hung those little black plastic bulls, that he gets from his red wine bottles, from the brim. Suppose that's his version of the Aussie bush hat with hanging corks. Inconspicuous he is not.

He's carrying the largest red canvas shoulder bag I've ever seen. It was packed full of books and plastic folders with newspaper clippings in. It means he walks lopsidedly too.'

'How do you know what was in the bag?'

'He kept rummaging around in his bag to find something and then jabbing his finger at the words for me to read them. If he wasn't pointing at something from his files he was writing phrases down on, like, a mini whiteboard for me to read. It was like having a conversation with Twitter although he was using less than forty characters rather than a hundred and forty. He's also got one of those red drawing toys, with the two white knobs, you know it makes stick drawings and shapes – it was in Toy Story. Anyway, he draws little pictures on it. For a man that can type quickly and has an iPad and iPhone which he could write messages on then his toys must be for effect.'

Steph was laughing: 'It might be quicker and it's safer. It's very unlikely that he's mad Nick. He'll be known in all the places he goes to in Malta. He's a friendly face - an eccentric, elderly writer on his last legs. Writers carry their research around with them. He probably has a poor memory. His world will be in that bag. What made you think he's weird?'

'For one thing, his apartment is a disgrace. For someone who used to tell us he was a domestic goddess, able to cook, clean and care for himself, he's gone downhill fast. He always said he loved ironing and, I've seen his party trick of neatly folding his gear into an outrageously small kit bag, whilst the rest of us were just chucking ours into our coffins. I don't think he's done any ironing or folding for a while looking at the scattered clothes and what he was wearing.

Just about every door, cupboard, drawer and wall in his apartment has post it notes on them. The post it notes on the drawers say what's in them. He probably doesn't have a drawer for socks as they seem to be scattered everywhere. There are corks, empty wine bottles, milk cartons, yoghurt cartons, plastic spoons … it's a mess. He's got a heap; you couldn't call it a shrine, like he had for Dusty Springfield, of books, magazines, photos, DVDs and CDs of Amy Winehouse on his dining table'.

5

'Worse, far worse,' Nick said with, for the first time a smile, 'he now watches every game Man U play in the outside bars. This is a Yorkshireman that's lived in London nearly all his life, so why would he start supporting Manchester United? He told me they only play well when Giggsy is playing. Did I want to know that?

He didn't make a sound all the time we were together and kept his scarf over his face. Afterwards I worked out what was different about him. He's clearly losing weight. He was always podgy – not anymore.'

'Does it matter what he looks like?' said Steph, softly.

'Well if he wanted to be the centre of attention he's succeeded. He looks and behaves like someone the Malta pulizija should stop and search his bag just because he's so weird. Then where would we be? He's spending money fast too. We walked around Sliema and we stopped for wine at three kiosks. He says he does the same walk every day. One old dear started pouring a half pint glass full of red wine as soon as she spotted Chris.

He gave them all a twenty euro note for our drinks and he let them keep the change. At one of the kiosks they gave him an envelope which he stuffed in his bag. He gave that kiosk owner a fifty euro note. You're right, they clearly love him over there but I found it bizarre. He asked me to tell you he loves you. There you are - I've told you'.

'Thanks Nick. It wasn't the most sensitively delivered romantic message I've ever had - but thanks. Chris is a good man he would never do anything which could hurt any of us, Nick, and….'

'He is, though Steph, I know he is. He's changed and not just physically. Loose cannons are dangerous. Why not go and see him yourself? I gave him your envelope. He says he'll be around for ages yet but I don't believe him. If the cancer doesn't get him the wine will'.

'Something must have happened to make you think that?'

'Two things come to mind. Firstly, he asked me to help him with his research – for him to ask me to help him so much is very unusual.'

'And what's the second thing? Then I've really got to get going Nick' Steph looked sideways at the wall clock. Nick saw her look and appreciating the long elegant curve of her neck, thought how very attractive she was. Her skin was the colour of strong coffee and her hair, although it was tied back looked as though its curl was not too tight. Nick bet she looked knock out when she wore it down.

Steph felt his eyes on her and curved her neck a little more. Even though she really did not like Nick very much she was very aware of her appeal to red-blooded males, and occasionally enjoyed teasing them with what they would never have.

'Well it's nothing he did more the company he's keeping. When we got to the restaurant in Valletta across from the Sliema ferry, there was a suited and booted, big gold watch, gold bracelet, Arab-looking gent - mid-fifties, I'd guess. He was with a young, probably Eastern European, tall, skinny, very classy, very pale, long blonde-haired woman who'd clearly been busy shopping. She had three or four designer shop bags. She may have been this guy's daughter but I don't think so. Chris pointed to a table for me to sit at and then went straight over to this couple.

He's always been a bit deaf but I think it's far worse now. I had to almost shout at him so it wasn't difficult for me to hear some of what this guy, let's say he was an Egyptian, this Egyptian said. Most of it was in another language, Greek, perhaps, I don't think it was Maltese and it wasn't Italian. The English words I heard him say were: 'Game', 'India' and 'Portal'. I agree I don't know the context – but it got my mind racing. He could have just been telling Chris a joke but no-one laughed. I suppose Chris couldn't laugh.

The only saving grace is that the Egyptian wasn't concerned about being overheard because close to them were two Maltese geezers, amongst the restaurant tables, fishing. Unbelievable!'

Now Steph was getting impatient, she knew it was a failing and had to bite her tongue to stop herself saying something cutting. Nick was beginning to waffle, and she wanted to go.

'OK, look, thanks Nick and for the message. Let's hope your imagination is running away with you. Chris is totally trustworthy. I don't think I'll be in contact with him though. He clearly doesn't want to hear from me and I really don't want to interfere with how he wants to see out his days. I'll tell the others. I've got to go, Nick. Ciao'.

Steph tapped the red Skype 'end call' button and Nick's face disappeared off the screen, his hand half raised in a wave and his mouth open - his farewell words lost in cyber space. Steph walked to the hall mirror and applied a clear lip-gloss, pursing her full lips together and then smiling back at herself. It was something that she had always done. The familiar image conjured up memories of specific occasions when she had stood in front of other mirrors, her first date, her graduation. Steph smiled as she shrugged her coat on, her mother had faxed everyone they knew in Jamaica, it had been a big day, the first of her family to get a degree.

The 'others' were the Chamberpots – the Lord Chamberlain's Men. Steph wasn't a Chamberpot but, she'd known them all for many years and thought of herself as an honorary member. Nick's main role in the Chamberpots was to give Chris information on the movements of certain VIPs and who they were meeting with.

3.

Trude snorted with laughter. A furtive glance down the carriage showed that she'd attracted the attention of her fellow passengers. Tears were now running down her cheek. She felt the need to blow her nose. She fumbled for and found a grubby looking hanky up her cardigan sleeve. The recollection that had caused this spontaneous eruption had sneaked up on her while she was gazing out of the window.

A young girl in an impossibly tight dress that barely covered her modesty sashayed past holding a cup of coffee with a sandwich balanced on top of it. She wobbled dangerously as she passed Trude. The train swayed, and the girl fought to stay upright on her impossibly high heels. Trude noticed a young man opposite leering at her and another older man watching her surreptitiously from behind his newspaper.

There had been a time when Trude drew such looks, but then she had not been giving it away. She bet the girl was. The danger of a coffee shower passed, Trude gazed out the window again.

At the week-end she had taken her mother, Pat, and Pat's two dearest friends out for lunch to a favourite pub just a few miles into the Derbyshire Dales. After lunch, they had adjourned for a final couple of proseccos. It was then that the following conversation took place

Pat: 'Do we have to get back at any time?'

Vi: 'Not for me but I'd appreciate being dropped off at the betting shop, the 2.30 came in for me.'

Lizzie: 'I thought I saw the smirk of satisfaction on your face while you were tucking into the rhubarb crumble and checking your iPhone.'

Pat: 'Eventually you had to win, Vi. What was it this time – a fave colour, a song title, the jockey's name reminded you of a hot lover – what made you back the horse?'

Vi: 'It was nothing of the sort. It was that my Bob, grouchy old git, said it stood absolutely no chance of winning. So, that made it a dead cert in my book. Anyway, I only bet a little bit. A pound each way or maybe a fiver. You've got to be careful, you know, it can run away with you.'

There was a moment's silence. Trude thought to herself that this betting lark often does run away with Vi and that Pat often lent her money at the end of the week. Then Vi said, 'Anyway we need some time to talk about Lizzie's fancy man. '

Pat: 'What? LIZZIE why is this the first I've heard about it?'

Lizzie: 'Oh, you know him? Old Steve – him that goes into the cafe. Well, I noticed he seemed to come in the cafe on the days I was on.'

Pat: 'And?'

Lizzie: 'And the other day he asked me if I'd like to go for a drink with him. I think I said, Why?'

Vi: 'As you do! My first thought exactly - Why?'

Lizzie: 'Well, just for, you know, companionship. He's on his own and he thought I was on my own too. It would be a drink and a chat and nothing more.'

Pat: 'And?'

Lizzie: 'Well we went to the Star. I've never paid much attention to him really. He's well spoken, certainly not scruffy but I noticed his hand shaking. I said, 'What's wrong with it'? and he said, 'a touch of Parkinson's.' and I thought to myself – that's what this is all about.'

Vi: 'Oh, Myyyyyyy God - not another one?'

Pat: 'You don't want to be bothering with all that.'

Vi: 'And he could last for Donkeys' years!'

It was Vi's 'Donkeys' years' remark that had made Trude snort. Moments later Trude was back to gazing out the window and wondering how her Lord Chamberlain's Men reunion would go. She remembered that at the end of the conversation in the pub garden Lizzie had said, 'Now Trude – do you ever hear from that friend of yours in Malta? You know the one with the throat cancer. Is he coping there on his own? Trude had no answer. Chris Hastings, the founder of the Lord Chamberlain's men was a complete mystery to her.

4.

Pup couldn't stop thinking about Charlie going to the O2 in a few days' time for the next Chamberpots' meet up and about the crap hand he'd been dealt which stopped him being there. He hadn't been to a Chamberpots meet up for years, in fact the last one he went to, he'd organised. Charlene Wright's presence, as a guest of Dave - the old dog - would have got him there any day but not this one. He had to go to work.

He yawned, put his fingers through a miscreant tangle of black hair that had fallen over his right eye. He nodded to the cat, which ignored him as it did every morning, and then he surveyed the breakfast debris all around him. Probably, around quarter past eight, Robbie Richardson, his youngest son would have flown out the door. The 'late-as-usual Richardsons' lived in Sunningfields Road in Hendon, North London. It would be stretching a point to say they lived together. Like ships passing in the night. Pup's son, Robbie, would never think of loading the dishwasher.

Pup went over to the biscuit tin and broke a Rich Tea in half. One half he ate. Then he walked over to the dog that also hadn't bothered, as usual, to greet him. The long haired, black, Bouvier remained stretched out, lying on his side, on an old, yellowing, smelly duvet cover that was inside a huge purple, badly gnawed, plastic dog basket. The dog's head was upright, thanks to its chin being rested on the side of this basket.

Monsieur Le Shag, nicknamed 'Mussy', had one big brown eye wide open. The other eye may have been open but it was hidden under his thick, wavy fringe. Mussy knew what was coming and was therefore feigning attentiveness even though he was nearly comatose.

Pup went down on his knees and pulled out both his pockets to show that there was nothing in them. He then showed Mussy that there was nothing up his sleeves. Finally, he showed Mussy that he had two completely empty hands. He then reached over Mussy's head with one hand and proceeded to pull half a Rich Tea biscuit from behind the dog's ear. Pup then gave the biscuit to Mussy, who gulped it down in an instant, and then, quite dismissively, closed his eyelids and resumed his sleep.

Pup sat down and moved aside a plate with some half-eaten pizza slices that his daughter, Zoe, had saved for breakfast from the night before. Clearly, what had been a good idea at midnight hadn't seemed so appealing to her at a quarter to eight in the morning. He filled a relatively clean bowl, probably his wife's, with Bran Clusters and poured on the last remaining drops of a carton of skimmed milk. He made a sort of clucking noise that was meant to convey to himself, the cat and the dog that he was unhappy with the state of the breakfast table.

Before he began to refuel Pup took eleven handwritten sheets and three press cuttings, from a large, crumpled envelope. The envelope had a Malta postmark. Pup knew that he should have destroyed the contents, and the envelope, days ago. He hadn't because this was the first letter he'd received from Chris in, at least, fifteen years.

The contents of the envelope deserved another reading. There was much hidden between the lines and in the cuttings but Pup hadn't cracked it all yet. He knew that he was being asked to do something big but he had to completely get onto Chris's wavelength before he could hope to fully establish the detail of his assignment.

Chris had clearly taken great care to ensure the bulky contents of the envelope would appear innocent to observers. However, Pup knew that Chris would feel he'd taken a risk in communicating directly by letter. Usually Pup was asked to do something for Chris by Dave. Face-to-face had been the only means of communication between the Chamberpots, until a month ago when Chris had broken his own rule by writing to Dave and now he'd broken the rule again by writing to Pup. Pup wouldn't tell the other Chamberpots about this letter.

Pup had been by far the youngest in the cricket team that Chris captained. At the time, he'd felt that many of his team mates regarded Chris as an old windbag. Yet, to Pup, Chris was the finest teacher and mentor that he could have wished for. Chris was almost the opposite in beliefs and disposition to his own, straight laced father. Chris always said that he thought his father, Geoff, was out of his time and resembled Dickens' descriptions of the professional classes.

Conversations with Chris were exciting. They discussed things that he wasn't studying at school, such as philosophy. Chris taught him how to explore reason, truth and concepts such as 'What is good?'; 'What is being?'; 'What is art?'; 'What is real and what is illusion?' Not just modern philosophers either, Chris was captivated by ancient Greek philosophers. He'd urged Pup to read articles written by the Chief Rabbi, Jonathan Sacks and a wonderful short book on the history of the world entitled 'Power and Greed' by Phillipe Gigantes.

12

This book divided the key influencers of the world into the Rule Makers, mainly good, and Grand Acquisitors, mainly bad. There were far more of the latter and Chris wanted far more of the former.

Chris, or 'Skip' as Pup often referred to him, thought the advent of platforms, artificial intelligence and machine learning could speed up the replacement of corrupt power seekers only interested in an elite few, with positive rule makers interested in the many. They allow hackers to hit as many targets as possible whilst reducing the risk to themselves.

Chris wasn't just a thinker though. He was an activist and passionate about changing society and righting wrongs. Most of his team mates thought Chris was probably too passionate about things and he shouted too much. This was caused by Chris' bad hearing, which continued to deteriorate over the years, and the copious quantities of red wine.

The drinking became a problem, more for Pup than Chris. Pup may have turned out to be a good cricketer, but most matches he played he was just pleased to get out of them alive. He'd always feel so bad during the match because of the drinking the night before. Then there was the pre-match pint and more pints at the tea interval, with a whisky chaser in cold weather. Then there was the heavy post-match session and drinking games with the opposition. This was followed by mandatory team bonding around midnight at their regular curry house in Mill Hill, accompanied by wine and brandy.

Of course, he could have said 'No' or asked for a Coke but he felt the peer pressure, especially when his father and Dave were in the team. It was too much for a teenager. By the time Pup got to Imperial, to do an ICT degree, he had a problem with the booze. Chris's drinking became even worse after his first wife, Sue, who he'd left but returned to nurse her, died. Chris seemed to start drinking red wine by the barrel. Even today, Pup would feel sick just thinking about the five dreaded words Chris would add to his invitation for them to meet up: 'Bring your thirst with you'.

The Chamberpots get-togethers in the early years were great because of the outstanding sporting events they attended together but they were often spoiled by the amount of alcohol consumed. The meal after the event was the worst bit of the day.

Trude, was always the top cat to Chris. In those days Trude was stunning and Dave fancied her like crazy, all the cricket team did. Trude always tried, but failed, to stop Chris and Dave encouraging the rest of them to drink so much. Trude prided herself on her worldliness, hell she more than anyone had seen it all, but she knew that sometimes she came over prudish, and that annoyed her, she was anything but, she just knew the devastation too much booze could do. Fortunately, years later, when Steph started coming to the get-togethers she became the second moderating influence. For this reason, Pup thought the Chamberpots get-togethers were better because of Steph being there.

Pup remembered when Chris's letter had arrived. It was the day after he'd seen Charlie for the third time. He'd first seen her, with Dave, when she was a little girl. Then recently, he'd seen her twice in quick succession. He knew his crush on her was crazy. Both recent times she'd been in a group of smart city types and she looked stand-out amazing.

She wouldn't have noticed him, of course, even though they'd been in touching distance of each other. He'd been working the tables. Charlie was often in the papers but Pup had found out where she lived and that she wasn't living with her husband. He knew where she worked now that she'd finished her tennis career. He was following her on Twitter but, for a celebrity, she wasn't very active and was unlikely to follow him - certainly not as a friend on Facebook or as a contact on LinkedIn. He hoped she'd look at his Twitter profile and be impressed by his nine thousand followers and then follow him back. But she hadn't. He'd worked out the age difference too. That bit wasn't so good. Her haughty head girl look was irresistible to Pup but he knew she was way out of his league in the 'likely to shag' stakes. Still a man could dream.

He comforted himself that anything up to a twenty-year age gap was quite acceptable today. Why, Tony Curtis had died leaving a wife who was thirty years younger than him. Michael Douglas has Catherine Zeta Jones. Rod Stewart will have some young model whose legs come up to his shoulders. Ronnie Wood too – likely all the Stones have. That Baldrick and Time Team actor guy probably doesn't reach the armpits of his younger partner. Do you need to be vertically challenged to get a young hot woman? Anyway…they all seem to be at it. That's show biz, folks.

Pup knew he was lean, tall, assisted dark and, some thought him, handsome. Certainly, the full head of hair and the lack of belly fat made him look much younger than his age. Hell, when he meets her it's not as though the first thing she'll ask is 'How old are you Mr Richardson?' Pup thought the biggest hurdles to him and Charlie falling madly in love might be that he had a wife and three kids and she didn't know who he was. Soon she would know who he was as Chris had asked him to invite her to a corporate product launch event he was working at.

Pup felt a definite hardening in his leisure shorts. He spooned in more bran clusters and looked again at the contents of the envelope. Reading his leader's words seemed like the best thing to do to take his mind off this unreachable woman of his dreams. Of course, as a last resort he could ask Dave what Chris's letter meant but this would be letting Chris down as he clearly didn't want Dave to know Pup's instructions. Chris regarded Pup as the smartest of the Chamberpots and so Pup felt it would be an insult to his intelligence and their friendship if he failed to work this out. 'Focus Pup – get it right'; he said to himself.

There were three cuttings, from the Malta Times a long while ago. Two cuttings were about fireworks, the third was about the Lockerbie bomb and the supposed culprit Mr Al-Megrahi. Pup had seen Al-Megrahi on television, not long before his death, at a meeting supporting Gadaffi, during the Libyan uprising.

The letter didn't refer to the cuttings at all. Each cutting gave Pup a task to achieve using technology and explosives. Pup was the techie in the Lord Chamberlain's Men. The letter started with the greeting 'Bonjour Jacques' and finished 'Au Revoir Jacques, Ernest Defarge'. The letter read like an essay on Chris's time in Malta. The uprisings in each of Malta's neighbours in North Africa and the Middle East were mentioned and Pup detected Chris's anger with US/NATO interventions and the lack of them in Syria. His reference to 'finding the medicine' was Chris's way of saying that if the Americans and

15

British want to start bombing to effect regime change they'll first invent a 'smoking gun' such as a chemical weapons attack, weapons of mass destruction and even a nuclear threat. Pup knew that his role was to use the darker side of the internet and social media to leak 'smoking guns' which would lead to the downfall of Chris's targets and allow new leaders in the regimes Chris wanted to change.

Chris's genuine interest in Anonymous and Luiz Security was joked about in the letter but it was in passing along with other comments on technology and gadgets. Chris and Pup had always talked technology and gadgets. The letter was mainly written as a description, to a friend, of what Chris had found were the best and worst things of him now living in Maltese society. This was an allegory for the good that needed to replace the bad in the USA and UK.

Pup realised that Chris's latest project was the most dangerous yet. It would put the Lord Chamberlain's Men's anonymity in jeopardy. Pup looked at his watch and realised he was running very late. He thought to himself one of the others can clear up the breakfast debris when they get back. After all, he hadn't created the mess.

5.

Dave Moore was sat on a bench in his front garden in Scarborough, North Yorkshire. He was wearing a blazer, v necked jumper, tie and grey, pleated trousers – his normal attire. He had just returned home from his golf club. There was a golf club just across the road from his house but Dave rarely played it as he deemed the members far inferior to those at his club. The quaint, old pub at the bottom end of his road, the Old Scalby Mills, was delightfully located at the seafront, with a stream, rock pools and a pedestrian bridge onto the Cleveland Way. Dave only frequented it on Christmas Day because tourists and his neighbour, a builder, were among the pub's clientele. All the spacious houses along Dave's road to the sea had large front and back gardens.

Dave had bushy grey eyebrows, grey-green eyes, a slight bony nose, long pointy ears, high cheekbones and slightly hollow cheeks with a small mouth and thin lips. Everything about the parts of Dave's body that were on show gave the impression of a man whose skin had been pinched rather too tightly. Apart from the face wrinkles there was no evidence of fat anywhere. This made Dave the envy of his peers and invited constant enquiries as to the state of his health. It annoyed them even more when he told them he'd never felt better.

Dave liked to position himself on this bench in his front garden as he could see through the front gate to the pavement and could admonish joggers, bicycle riders and dog walkers for any of their indiscretions. Dave had bought vintage sports cars over the years, which enhanced the cache of his front driveway on fine days. His current pride and joy was a 1946 Jaguar SS 100. Dave was always immaculately dressed. He felt he was always on duty. He was regularly photographed for the local media, with the Scarborough elite, attending fund raising events for charities and community causes. He gave the impression to everyone that he was the life and soul of the party and a prosperous and generous man.

Dave was reading the letter Chris had sent him. He'd read it again tomorrow when he was travelling to London for the Lord Chamberlain's Men day out. Dave had instructions to give them. Then he'd destroy the letter. Dave was Chris's oldest friend, they'd been together at school – Beverley Grammar School – and been in London at the same time when doing their degrees. It was in London that they played cricket for the same team which led to the founding of the Lord Chamberlain's Men.

Dave was enjoying his regular trips to London to meet with various contacts of Chris but it wasn't so much the people he met that gave him pleasure but having access to Chris's clubs and credit cards. Dave didn't hate the Establishment or the UK being the 51st State of America in the same way Chris did but he never let on. Chris had said for the last thirty years that the UK and the US would soon have white supremacists as PM and President. Dave would never say to Chris that he was in favour of England being solely for the English.

Dave felt that the Iraq invasion combined with the financial sector crash and bail outs had been the tipping points that escalated Chris's activism and moved it from just being focused on British targets. Then there was Michael Moore's documentary 'Bowling for Columbine'.

Chris would rant about the impotence of the GPs' campaign for an inquiry on Kelly's alleged suicide and the failure of human rights groups regarding Guantanamo Bay and Bradley Manning's incarceration, without trial. Dave's view was that Chris should 'Get a life'.

Dave had known Chris's loathing for the US, which had now reached epic proportions had always been bubbling underneath even twenty years ago when he'd been an HR Director at a US multinational. Chris had labelled himself, to Dave, as a 'Hire, Fire, and Settle Professional'. Even then Chris had felt implicated in the rich getting richer. He understood excess and what City Boy and City Girl revealed about the big swinging dicks and the incompetence of the guys at the top with the fat bonuses. Chris knew and loathed all the lobbyists from The City of London Corporation to the Taxpayers Alliance. Dave would smile in agreement at Chris's rants but thought him a fool not to go with the flow. Early retirement hadn't come too soon for Chris. Dave despised Chris.

Chris would argue that you fight evil propaganda with good propaganda and replace the bad guys with the good guys. Dave thought life was too short – what's done is done. It was only the money, Chris's wealth, that kept their friendship together.

Dave thought Chris saw himself as the English Michael Moore. 'Who supplied the highly trained and experienced pilots? How did each tower collapse? Why did Bush say he'd seen the plane fly into the first building on a telly, outside the classroom he was waiting to go into? No-one had seen that bit live on TV, as those video pictures weren't on air until the next day.' Why are the US Drones massacring targets plus civilians, every day, from a base in Saudi Arabia? On and on he'd go. Dave felt it was megalomania – no just sick - for Chris to think he could get the answers to these questions and, anyway, 'Who gives a shit?'.

Outrageously, to Dave, Chris believed that Saddam, Gadaffi and Bin Laden will have been tortured before they died. They knew too much having been funded by, and even trained by the US, that the manner and all the media content on their deaths will have been staged. Stooges, lookalikes, films after the event – all these were certainties in Chris's world. He didn't care about them being killed it was just that he took the mainstream media propaganda as a personal insult. Same with the major corporates running governments and major institutions. He hated FIFA and the International Olympics Committee as much as Government for the inexorable pursuit of wealth and power so the rich get richer and the poor stay poor. Chris thought in the same way that bribes and bungs bought votes for which country staged the World Cup or the Olympics, that a minority Government would even use bribes and bungs to buy politicians votes to stay in power. Dave's view was that Chris was 'One sad bastard'.

Dave thought it poetic justice that Chris could no longer rant about all this, since his last surgery in Malta. Silence is golden.

Dave was amused that it was entirely his own fault that Chris had formed the Chamberpots to get rid of the bad guys. Dave had just been trying to impress the attractive wife of a miner, during the strike in 1984, when he said to Chris: 'We must do summat about it'.

Dave could still picture the miner's wife. Pint glass in front of her, cigarette always poised within inches of her lips – pink lipstick. Slim, tall, light jeans, brown leather boots, black top, blonde, frizzed, shoulder length hair and a hard woman, no doubt, but she was amazing looking. Thankfully, for self-preservation, Dave thought, nothing happened. Mind, she was the one that told us that all the miners' phones were tapped. The miners proved it by sending the police on wild goose chases. It was a lesson learned and why the Chamberpots, until Dave received this letter, had only ever communicated face to face.

Dave knew that Chris felt this was his final project. Chris dying of cancer was the opportunity for Dave to make a financial killing.

19

After all, Chris had money to burn and some very wealthy contacts. Chris was already paying Dave handsomely to do meetings in London. Dave was particularly enjoying using the Institute of Directors magnificent buildings in Pall Mall as his London base - courtesy of Chris's cards.

At his rugby, cricket and tennis clubs his fellow members thought Dave was well off. After all he had a good pension, some inherited money from his and his wife's parents and a nice detached house in one of the most sought-after areas.

However, Dave's every penny had gone into keeping up appearances. He had no savings. For the last eighteen years he'd been paying at least a quarter of his income into the account of an Orange Lodge in Scotland. This arrangement had been made by the late Geoff Richardson, a Chamberpot, and fellow Chamberpot Pup's Dad.

To Dave it felt like blackmail but Geoff had regarded it as a fair price to pay to buy silence. The loan had covered a sizeable pay off. Geoff had never told him whether Geoff's son, Pup, knew about this arrangement. It was not the sort of thing that Dave would ever bring up in conversation with Pup.

Dave resented that he hadn't enough money to really enjoy his retirement. He would use Chris's loss of speech to his maximum advantage. He'd started to dream of a better life from a new location and with a new identity. There'd be horse racing in Dubai and golf in Florida. His wife, Gill, would not be a part of his future. Gill would go into care.

6.

Matt Robinson and Ricky Sharpe looked like a comedy duo as they stood playing a slot machine at the Chequers pub in Hendon. It was a work day for both these business owners. Matt, or 'Tricks' as he was known to the other Chamberpots, and Ricky, or 'Scalesy' to the Chamberpots, were in their branded uniforms. The logo of Tricks' gym was on a red and white Nike tracksuit and Scalesy's plumbing firm logo was on a black waistcoat and black tie – he looked like a snooker player. Tricks with his towsly, peroxide blonde hair towered over Scalesy and looked twice the width of his neatly coiffured, dapper friend. They were both well-known characters but no-one in the pub would disturb their private conversation as they slotted coins into the flashing and beeping machine.

Scalesy: 'Do you remember when we used to go with Chris and Dave to the Chinky around the corner?

Tricks: 'Sure do Scalesy, the lunchtime special and it was usually Hot and Sour soup and then Sweet and Sour Pork with egg fried rice in a Tupperware bowl'.

Scalesy: 'And all served at our table by the inscrutable Odd Job who I bet was bigger than you'.

Tricks: 'Not as mobile though and not as good at gambling either. If his horses or dogs weren't coming in he'd almost throw the plates as us. That was normal, in fact the only time I remember him winning big was when Chris tipped him that horse at Newmarket – Caravaggio'.

Scalesy: 'And it was the scene of many a bizarre conversation between Odd Job and our leader. The Skip was always trying to teach him useful English expressions such as 'Has anyone ever accused you of 'putting a foot wrong' or 'putting your foot in it' to which Odd Job would reply 'No ray, nor ter my norredge'.

Tricks: 'Brilliant. I remember one day after Odd Job had drunk about a gallon of Carling, because he drank more than any of the customers, he said to Chris: 'Jus corr me 'Misser Reeewhyabul' and Chris said, 'Why should I call you Mister Reliable, Odd Job?' and Odd Job shouted, 'Cos I nerra purra foot wong, innit?'.'

Scalesy: 'Odd Job was a genius and he gave Chris as good as he got. Do you remember he persuaded Chris to make a visit to his mate who was a tattooist?'

Tricks: 'Like yesterday, Chris wanted us all to go to be tattooed with a Chamberpots symbol. We told him to fuck off and that as the leader he should take one for the team and get it done first. If it looked alright, then we'd all get it done'

Scalesy: 'Fortunately, it was rubbish'

Tricks: 'Chris was probably Odd Job's mate's first customer'

Scalesy: 'His masks of comedy and tragedy on his neck looked like they'd been drawn in a black felt pen by a three-year-old.'

Tricks: 'Hilarious. Mind you, it was well inked – it's still there. Fucking Dave never stopped taking the piss out of Chris's tattoo'

Scalesy: 'Right, I'd better get back to work. I don't like checking on my guys because I do trust them but I know the thought of me checking keeps them on their toes'.

Tricks: 'I trust no-one. Here's the gear for Dave to get to Chris'

Tricks handed Scalesy a small white envelope.

'Thanks Tricks. This is dangerous stuff we're now doing for the Skip. I don't like it. I'm to give it to Pup who is going to hide it in something and then Pup will give it to Dave when he sees him in town'.

7.

Chris put down his Cross-gold fountain pen. He put the magnetic clasp around the leather-bound book with gold leaf trim that he'd been writing in. He placed the book in the front pocket of his canvas bag on the seat next to him. After leaving Nick in Valletta he'd gone back to Upper Barrakka Gardens, changed his clothes in the public conveniences, carefully stacked all the files and props he'd been using with Nick into a locker and then taken a white taxi from the rank outside.

The taxi had taken him to Virtu Ferries where he'd caught the late afternoon catamaran to Sicily. It was a ninety-minute crossing which Chris made quite often.

The seats on the high-speed catamaran were like comfortable, wide, first class, airline seats but as usual, there were far more people being sick than in a plane. In the side block, there was no-one within three rows of him. He could now; unobserved, open the package Nick had given him.

In the package were three envelopes and a small packet. Chris had always enjoyed opening presents. He had a process for unwrapping to ensure he didn't rip the wrapping paper. He'd then fold the wrapping paper neatly, ready for future use. He loved prolonging the anticipation. This, he thought, must be how prisoners or soldiers feel when they receive a present from home.

The first envelope that he opened contained a Roger Federer, red tennis sweat band and a postcard with a picture of the Eiffel Tower. It was from Steph and he'd look forward to reading it later when he was back in his apartment. He had fond memories of their week-end escapes to Paris.

The second envelope mainly contained diagrams, none of which made too much sense to Chris but he could give it to someone to whom it would. The diagrams were of the plumbing in a yacht. That envelope was from Scalesy.

The third envelope was from Dave containing a short progress report from the meetings that Chris had asked him to carry out in London. The progress report was only understandable to Chris. To anyone else it would have been an update on the new additions to Dave's collection of old football programmes.

Chris hoped the fourth packet contained something from Pup and Tricks. He was relieved to find that it did. Inside were three small silver cups and some tiny red sponge balls. Chris pinched each of the balls between his forefinger and thumb. The second ball that he pinched had a hard centre. He slotted everything, including the folded packaging, neatly into his bag.

CHAPTER TWO: Missing in Action

Enthusiast: deeply involved in something, especially a hobby

1.

NICK BURGESS WAS EXHAUSTED. Even travelling business class was a chore. He was out of shape, breathing heavily and his rather puffy cheeks were always flushed. It was probably high blood pressure but Nick wouldn't see a doctor.

He'd see a dentist to keep his teeth pearly white, an optician to ensure perfect rimless spectacles for his blue eyes, a hairdresser to keep his short silver hair nicely layered, a cosmetic clinician for Botox and a tailor to ensure his dark suits hid his paunch as much as possible. But he wouldn't see a doctor. They may have bad news for him. They may prescribe treatment or time off work.

Nick could not afford any time off work and any suggestion that he was undergoing any treatment might be just the excuse his boss needed to start moving him out. It's the same as pro team sports. You play with an injury because you're afraid if you miss a game someone else will take your place permanently. After this trip, he'd get less than two days at home before it was time to fly out again. He was walking from the cab into Chicago O'Hare airport. Ouch! A hand had been clamped hard and tight, pinching his shoulder bone. Before he could re-act he heard:

'Nicky Boy what a pleasant surprise this is. Bud, we can have a little chat. Keep walking, turn left and jump into the Merc.'

'But I've got a flight'

'No problem. This won't take long, bud'

Nick's bag and suitcase were taken from him and the door of the dark green Mercedes was opened by a sharply dressed, middle aged, brunette who greeted him with a kiss and said

'Nick – hey we've missed you'

The man whose hand on Nick's shoulder had guided him there was now sat beside him. Small, stocky, dark suited, short grey hair, grey goatee and much gold on show – Rolex, cufflinks, bracelet and ear stud. The brunette was his wife.

'How was HQ, Nicky Boy?'

'Cool. You'll know we're all set for the Czech Republic and Poland and …'

'No need to say more. We should talk about that'

'But you're doing well I've seen your stats. And I'll bet the numbers I see aren't even a fifth of what you're raking in. Am I right?' said Nick

'Times are hard Nicky Boy. Austerity is the name of the game in Europe. Good for recruitment but bad for how much the recruits can afford to invest. It's no good to you either. You won't get promoted on sales of starter kits'

'Where would I get promoted to, Richard?'

Richard King looked out the window. There was nothing to see. The Mercedes was and would remain stationary. His eyes had not yet contacted Nick's. Nick had noticed before that when Richard King was about to confront Nick, or any other Supramax Life executive, he had a habit of fiddling and twisting his gold bracelet. He was fiddling and twisting right now. He turned to look Nick straight in the eye.

'What we need, Nicky Boy is a new marketing plan for Europe. We desperately need increased incentives for the leadership. You need strong down lines internationally now. There's big competition and you know it. I've laid it out in here'

Richard King handed Nick a red memory stick and continued:

'It gives you the complete business case and a power point. Present it. Present it as your idea to the Board and the Owners. It'll cost seven-point six mill dollars in year one, to the leadership, but each year after that the additional cost will be six mills for each hundred mills at retail. Makes good business sense, bud, there's no doubt about it. You'll be a hero.'

'No way. You know I can't do that Richard. It's not a year since the last change'

'We don't use the word 'can't'. This is an opportunity. What's the mission of the corporate staff at Supramax Life?'

'Freedom, Family, Hope and Success helping all independent business owners to achieve their personal and business goals' – but this is still crazy. The Owners wouldn't even let me get it on a board agenda. European Vice President isn't at the top of the corporate tree, you know, and I'm only just hanging on to my branch as it is.'

'You won't think that Nicky Boy when you see what's on that memory stick. Neither you nor the Founders need to upset me. The Founders are more into politics now than business – it'll make sense to them. In fact, when you see the presentation and hand-outs I've done for you – you'll see that it'll do great things for your career. '

'I'm sorry Richard, this time I really can't. They'll think I've lost my marbles....'

As Nick handed the memory stick back, Richard's strong hands closed Nick's fingers back around it. 'You will keep it. There's a little report from one of my people too. It's a bonus feature. The report suggests that Rosie Charlton did not commit suicide voluntarily.'

Richard turned away to look out the window again and then said calmly but softly:

'In fact, there's evidence that you lied at the inquest. You knew that your Regional Manager was there the day she died. You wouldn't want me to let that journalist that's on your case, what's his name....?

'Pete Bryan' said Nick

'You wouldn't want me to let Pete Bryan have it to put on his website, would you?'.

Silence.

Richard turned to look Nick in the eye again and said:

'We'd better get going and you've a plane to catch. How about we have a KIT in London next week and you can give me your action plan on how you're going to persuade the Founders?'

2.

The letter Chris wrote to Dave:

A surprise missive from your oldest friend,

No-one should worry, when they get to our age, about being so beneath the radar that folk can't even remember whether we're dead or alive. If we're lucky we may be remembered as old do-gooders. We're better than that but our contributions will always remain anonymous – you can count on me.

I've a bone to pick with you, Dave. When I asked what women get out of having your prick in their bottom I was referring to anal sex, not what you described. That's 'Spoons' to me. Every porn film seems to go two mins blowing, two mins licking – cunnilingus is a reet funny old word, eh? Two mins doing doggy - that always makes me laugh too, two mins on cow girl, two mins on reverse cow girl and then, what seems like, the next 2 days on anal sex. What's all that about?

I wouldn't care if it was only porn but I've met blokes who say they love it. I'm reliably informed that butt plugs are top sellers. Why? If you're gay then there are fewer options but still - can you see what the guy underneath gets out of it? Did you know that Eskimo men choose their women based on how fat they are, with the fatter women being the most desirable? They're interested in keeping warm, you see. So, they choose on girth. I suppose they sleep under their wife, instead of a duvet.

So, let's get back to Spoons. To be crystal clear, I don't mean the stirring or supping kind of spoon but the arm around the waist, other hand cupping her breast, knees bent, all points connected – her back and my front sort of melded together.

'Spoons' is a big, all-time favourite memory – back in the day. It's eleven in the morning and Sue and I have still got hangovers. Hell! I used to drink snakebites then - remember? We're weak from laughter and making love. We don't give a damn about what we should be doing and we may stay in bed 'til tea-time the next day.

Then one of us will raid the meter and pop out to the deli down the road to get some bread rolls, a huge lump of his finest mature Canadian cheddar and a bottle of Frascati. Funny, I can't see the point of white wine now. The wine and cheese rolls were the finest meal we could have - perking us up in more ways than one.

Do you use those blue pills or have you no need? I'm not sure that I have the need. I was still OK with 'Happy Endings' last time I went to a Thai massage parlour over here. I felt a bit old, sad and silly and don't think I'll bother any more. Tricks is the man for the pills methinks – when you need them. Find out when you next see him. I think 68 is a good enough age to give up sex out of decorum and good taste – don't you? Nah, you wouldn't.

Anyway, the smoke and musky smell in the room would get smokier and muskier. The sun streaming in through the holes in the curtains turned to darkness again and we'd stay in bed until at least the next lunchtime.

Cor 'Eck, Dave, I'm turning myself on here. No wonder I married Sue. Of the two goes I've had at marriage the one with Sue made the most sense because of the sex. Bet we'd still be married if we'd had kids and I hadn't made a few little mistakes along the way. My wanting to go and live with Trish didn't help things. Of course, there's never any future in men-women relationships. I'm surprised we keep trying. In fact, Scalesy is the only one of all of us that you could call 'happily married'. I suppose plumbers get a little extracurricular activity on their visits to customers' homes or in Scalesy's case on his visits to swanky mansions and yachts.

Women will always be a complete mystery to men. The pursuit of hedonism is not possible if there's a relationship with a woman involved. One minute they're eating, drinking, laughing and playing in bed with their toes curling up and down, in sheer contentment, then, out of the blue, just as you're falling asleep they'll ask you a trick question. A question to which there is just no answer you can give that won't turn the warmth into black ice. Questions like; 'you don't like my hair short, do you?'; 'which meal would you really fancy at your mother's?', 'which of your previous partners were the best in bed and why?'; 'if it was a choice between winning the lottery and having me, which would you choose?' A moment's hesitation or deviation or an 'aw let me sleep' and you are dead in the water.

BTW the sex I was describing is now termed 'hot vanilla' and my extra-curricular exploits would now be termed 'polyamory' – the practice of simultaneous relationships as a way of keeping your primary relationship vibrant and healthy – who knew? Mind, you're meant to get the agreement of all the parties. If only someone had told me the rules. I blame the pill – it encouraged men to be irresponsible. We never even thought about condoms. Life was just one big love in.

You, Scalesy, Tricks and Pup deliberately twist everything I say just to wind me up. But I blame you more than them. Anyone looking at me and you see two old farts. They look at us with disdain. They think that by sixty we've lost the right to be of interest as individuals but that we're part of some community of neutered squatters that all look the same and are just whiling away the hours until

29

we're moved on. How many times have I been mistaken for you when we're sat together? From the back, we're identical twins.

Anyway, I won't be sodomising anyone but likely you will. I started and will finish in nappies. Even with designer incontinence pads I'm not going to be a sex magnet. So, I need your opinion on anal sex from the woman's point of view – it's for an article I'm doing. My piggy bank is hungry. Just a few paragraphs will do – a testimonial, if you like - anonymous of course.

Mind, you've probably done more of all this stuff than I have because you got off to a better start at the poly – 'uni' now, Dave. What was the female to male ratio at Trent Park? Was it six to one? It certainly scrambled your brain. For at least four years you were a robotic, seek and score machine leaving damp patches and tear stains throughout North London.

I'm gutted that I won't be with you at our Chamberpots get together. Not as gutted as I am about missing the Olympics in nine months' time – that's the once in a lifetime opportunity that will pass me by. I enjoyed the tennis last year and whenever it's Trude's turn then it's always fab.

When you're at the tennis could you pass on to Trude, Pup, Scalesy and Tricks my next 'Top Ten, All Time, Sporting Greats'? I'm counting on you all to help with my collection of memorabilia.

Nick's here in Malta soon so I'll tell him the list myself. So, the list is

1. TB
2. WH
3. SB
4. PW
5. DC2
6. NM
7. PM
8. LC
9. RI
10. FST

There must be a chance that Number 6 will visit his niece, Charlene Wright, soon. Of course, he's so famous now his minders may not let you get close?

I've enclosed a job advert for you. They come up from time to time. So, if you're serious about Malta next summer? The Fondazzjoni Wirt Artna, the

*Malta Heritage Trust, is looking for full time and part time tour guides. That's
you — sound knowledge required of Maltese and International military history —
you can get away with that too.*

*Here is better than America, Dave. Everywhere in Europe, North Africa
and the Middle East are easily accessible. If you enjoy it half as much as I have
then you'll be a very happy lad. In the meantime, thanks for doing the London
trips. Take care, my old mate.*

3.

Charlie saw her friend, Gail, walking back to their table. She was
carrying a tray with a bowl of soup, a small tuna salad, a bottle of
Evian, and a mini bottle of Pinot Grigio – all to be shared. 'Well, have
you decided?' Gail said, as she unloaded the tray. Charlie felt herself
blushing. Hopefully, she thought, no-one, including Gail, will notice.

Charlie was tall and slim and had an athletic body that was much
admired. She had a small roundish face which always had a little red
triangle in each cheek. The little red triangles were more obvious when
she blushed. To Charlie they felt like the little red 'do not cross' men
flashing away at pedestrians on zebra crossings. Experience taught her
not to worry as most people's attention was drawn to her large blue-
green eyes, underneath a startlingly black, fringe.

Gail had left Charlie to grab a table at the café in Covent Garden,
while she got the food. Gail's parting words had been 'At least one of
them must go – you can't have three of them at the same time. By the
time I get back I want to know which one, or preferably two, you're
going to ditch?'

Charlie was vacillating between feeling smug that she could have
three lovers at once, and feeling guilty. She sometimes wondered if her
promiscuousness had something to do with the fact that she had been
a gangly, wiry haired wholly unattractive teen with acne that worked

as a very effective repellent to the opposite sex. But as the acne had dried up, and her body had caught up with her over long limbs, she had emerged a butterfly attracting butterfly catchers wherever she went. Gail had fixed her with a steely gaze and Charlie widened her eyes slightly.

'Don't try that with me sister!' Gail said and Charlie began to pick at the eyelashes of her right eye as though she had been blinking because of something in her eye. Not many people rattled her confidence but Gail was one of them.

Gail was imposing. She was always intense despite being quite pretty – small, voluptuous and slim, pixie like face with fine, shoulder length blonde hair, piled high. She was power dressed in a light grey suit and russet blouse which was quite a contrast with Charlie's all black - boots, skinny jeans and short jacket over a red roll neck top.

Both young women were an advert for wealthy, healthy living and the best in couture. Dolce & Gabbana, Alexander McQueen, Philip Treacy, Chloe, Christian LeBouten and Jimmy Choo featured in their wardrobes. Both would have been comfortable with the other guests if they had been invited to the Royal Wedding, as some of their friends were. Everything they were wearing was very 'now'.

Despite being the same age as Charlie, Gail's career and independently earned income was way ahead. Gail co-owned a successful PR consultancy and corporate speaker bureau. Charlie knew that she'd have to answer the question now that Gail had returned:

'It's complicated...' started Charlie, her long eyelashes sweeping the top of her flushed cheeks.

'Madness' interrupted Gail

'It's complicated by Andy wanting to leave his wife. He wants me to leave Graeme so that we can live together and..... not where we are...'

'Where?'

'I don't know but not in Yorkshire, certainly not Yorkshire - and he's in a hurry.'

'Like, how much in a hurry?'

'Like days. He's not worried about losing his job …. I doubt whether the club cares either way. He's pissed about not getting clearance to be with the VIPs. Gail, he's desperate and he's violent.'

'Ditch him. He'll wreck everything, Charlie. It starts by you keeping your legs shut.'

Charlie flushed deeper, now she felt more guilty than smug. She dropped her teaspoon with a clatter onto her saucer and said;

'It's so fucking unfair. I love what Yorkshire could do for me. I don't know why Uncle Dave is helping me so much but this is my big chance. Andy looked fantastic when we first met. Now he looks like shit - probably having a breakdown or something. I know for a fact that he owes more people than me money. Money he's probably blown on numbers 17 and 35. The bit that scares me rigid is that I don't think he's read the rule book about not hitting women'.

'What about Mike?'

'Whatever. Mike's not an issue, never will be. I'll see Mike now and again. God Gail, I've known Mike since our first day at Uni. The chat, sex, whatever is all cool. I stayed at his place last night. Gail, it's just so good to see you and to be back in London, even as a day tripper. Wish I'd stayed with Mike rather than marry Mr. Boring.'.

'Get over it. Go to the police. I don't think you ever were the marrying kind Charlie'

'Too late though, now isn't it? I'll work something out but I am scared Gail and …. Look we need to finish this because I've got to meet these grumpy old men and women at the O2 in under an hour. Must admit, I'm really, really looking forward to the tennis. When you're back at your office could you text me with the deal on that social media, speaker guy - I think we could book him?'

4.

Trude had always looked forward to a day out without her mother. Today was extra special as she'd organised the Chamberpots get together from top to toe. As a bonus, she'd end the day with a few hours of Steph's company on the train journey back to Sheffield.

Just walking through St Pancras was thrilling to Trude. She thought it was one of the very best renovation projects she had ever seen. She loved the sculptures, the light, the cavernous space, the arches, the big clock, the champagne bar next to the Euro shuttle, the colourful shops and cafes – it was all quite magical. Walking through St Pancras station was a lovely way to start a day in London. She had felt differently when she worked in the Capital, but now she could enjoy being there, enjoy the veneer of affluence and not think about the grimy underbelly of the city.

After a moment's reflection, Trude concluded that the recent building of the parade and fountains outside Sheffield station was a damned good bit of renovation too. Trude was intensely proud of everything to do with her county, Yorkshire. Although she lived in London for many years, now she was back in the North, she found it hard to give the southerners credit for anything.

Trude and her mother were minor celebrities in Yorkshire as they attended every home game of both Sheffield United football club and Yorkshire County Cricket Club. They looked like mother and daughter. They both wore glasses, never contact lenses. Trude was taller and heavier. Trude never really did anything with her straight, golden once but white now, hair. She just scrunched it under her Blades beanie for trips to Bramall Lane and under her wide brimmed Yorkshire CCC sun hat for matches at Headingley. Trude and her mother, Pat, both showed their support of their teams by wearing replica shirts but they wore different headgear. Pat's immaculate perm was covered by the various headscarves she wore, in the team colours.

Pat certainly had the loudest voice of the two of them and there wasn't a footballer, cricketer or official that hadn't been given some of her expert advice. Astonishingly, to Pat, her advice never seemed to be followed. This may have been because when shouting at sporting venues both her accent and her expressions became somewhat opaque. Each sentence ended in the words 'you big aporth'.

Trude and Pat were more famous at the cricket than the football. This was due to the security personnel at Headingley, presumably forewarned by their superiors, allowing Trude through the turnstiles along with a large shopping trolley bag. She dragged this bag behind her from her home in Sheffield onto the free city bus, onto the train at Sheffield station, back onto the train at Leeds station and then off the train at Burley Park station and all the way to her seat in the members' stand.

In this trolley bag was delicious fodder that had taken at least two hours for Trude and Pat to prepare. Large flasks of hot and cold drinks, appropriate for all weather conditions, were also in the 'packing up', as Pat called it. The hot, milky coffee was a favourite as it was laced with whisky. Trude and Pat would feed and water many grateful members in their vicinity throughout the day's play. Not surprisingly it was a rule in the members' stand that all would ensure that, whatever time Trude and Pat arrived, that their usual four seats would be available to them. They needed four seats as they were both quite large women and they also needed space to unpack.

Trude and Pat were following a tradition. When Pat's father had died she had taken her father's season ticket and place and accompanied her mother to watch the games at Bramall Lane and Headingley. When Pat's husband, Trude's father, died then Trude had happily agreed to accompany Pat. Trude, an only child, had neither been married nor had children so this tradition would die with her. In the meantime, the Yorkshire members intended to make the most of it.

Most Yorkshire members watching a four-day game of cricket on a week-day are elderly, retired and don't have the money to spend in the club's splendid bars, cafés and restaurants. Watching the cricket outdoors was certainly preferable to many of the alternatives.

Sometimes Trude had imagined attending the cricket with a child, a boy, a perfect mix of her and Chris, his hair slicked down and his eyes bright as he watched the wickets fall. She would imagine him turning to her looking up at her in anguish or delight as fortunes changed and his eager young hands reaching out to catch a ball hit for six and heading their way. Trude reprimanded herself for imagining a boy, the child could just as easily have been a girl, but try as she might, the stereotype had a hold of her.

A boy it was, or rather wasn't. Trude had noticed that as she got older some tendrils of regret were threatening to climb her subconscious like a determined ivy. She did not want to be regretful of anything, it served no purpose, and she realised that way madness lay.

One of the indoors alternatives to the day at Headingley for some of the elderly gang of Yorkshire members was sitting in an armchair, in a circle, in a very warm old people's home with the smell of urine and disinfectant in the nostrils. Worse than the erratic conversation from those with and without Alzheimer's, in the circle, was when their babble was interrupted by the staff's regular 'tellings off'.

These 'tellings off,' addressed to your first name, were shouted using a tone and vocabulary more appropriate for admonishing a toddler. Breakfast, lunch and dinner were just the same in terms of social discourse but would be accompanied by tasteless food and medication. For those living in such 'homes', who had no cooking facilities of their own, Trude and Pat provided a dream opportunity to sample proper home-made fayre.

A constant stream of grateful friends came to sit next to them through the day. Each visitor was guaranteed one, or all, of a knowledgeable chat, laughter, a cup of tea, a beef and mustard sandwich, pork pie, sausage roll, hard-boiled egg and a slice of Pat's, famous throughout the Broad Acres, Parkin cake.

Many of the more well-to-do of the Yorkshire members disapproved of Trude and Pat's demeanour. However, those that had chosen in the past to confront them had been surprised by how articulately they were out-argued. Trude and Pat were graduates and professionals in music and librarianship, respectively. They were strongly and vocally supported by the clear majority of the members' stand. The establishment had decided it was not wise to admonish Trude or Pat on anything.

Trude was worried about Chris. She knew that the journey back to Sheffield would include a gentle interrogation by Steph as to what Trude knew about Chris's plans. All the Chamberpots suspected that Trude and Chris had been an item at some stage. Neither Trude, nor Chris, had ever confirmed this.

Trude had not let the Chamberpots know that Chris never asked her to do anything to help him with his list of targets. In fact, she never bothered to keep a record of the lists Dave gave to her. She couldn't let on that she was treated differently as the others might draw conclusions. Chris had always confided in her but never asked her advice. But if the Chamberpots knew what she knew, they'd never believe that he wasn't influenced by her. He wasn't, he was just someone who never wanted to upset anyone and so he ended up making bad decisions that caused great upset. Trude was the only Chamberpot that knew Chris had left his wife Sue to live with Trish because Trish was pregnant. Trish miscarried so Chris never had children. He'd have been a good father. Trude would never say anything to alienate her oldest and closest circle of friends.

Sometimes Trude felt that she was living someone else's life, or that she was directing players in a play. Even her relationship with her mother sometimes seemed like they were not related and at other times as though they were the same person. The thought of Chris dying sometimes felt as though she was anticipating his decline without emotion and at other times she felt like the end of Chris was the end of life as she knew it. It brought her own inevitable demise, and that of her mother into sharp focus.

Trude knew that people would be surprised if they knew about her secret thoughts and the sometimes-black moods that she struggled with. She had cultivated her capable persona well, hell she did not have to cultivate it, she was it. But like an onion, she had many layers that she was careful to keep hidden. The only person who truly knew her was Chris. Not even her mother knew of the demons that she wrestled with from time to time. That would cause her mother suffering and Trude would never do that. It was not as though she poured her heart out to Chris, more that he just knew.

Trude had not been surprised that Chris and Steph had got together. She liked Steph a lot and could see why Chris had fallen for her. The only time that Trude had felt very envious of Steph was when Chris had taken Steph on holidays abroad and week-ends in Paris. Trude hadn't been abroad for many years, ever since her father died and she would have loved to relax with someone who knew her as well as she knew herself. Every year her mother insisted on an autumn break in the Lakes or the Highlands and an early spring break in Swanage. All their breaks were planned to ensure that not a game was missed at Bramall Lane or Headingley.

5.

Pup walked in to the Euston Flyer with a huge smile and a spring in his step. He loved getting together with Tricks and Scalesy. They didn't do it very often and today would be a quick get together before he went to work and they went off to the O2. Their conversations usually started with football but quickly moved on to the targets on Chris's team sheet. They discussed why the targets were on the team sheet and what kind of information they could get to help Chris make those targets 'disappear up their own arse' or 'impotent', as Chris termed it. Now they were all taking orders from Dave and were being asked to do more than ever before. They needed to compare notes before Scalesy and Tricks saw Dave at the Chamberpots get-together. Pup wouldn't tell them about the letter he'd received from Chris.

'Hey, look what the cat's dragged in Scalesy. Late as usual and neatly avoiding buying the round. Here's your Coke, Pup – we've got pints of ESB which you owe us next time' said Tricks.

Pup grabbed his Coke from the high, circular table, next to the slot machine, which Scalesy and Tricks were standing at. The pub was crowded, noisy and the big screen had Sky Sports News on it. It was just the way that Pup, Scalesy and Tricks liked their meeting venues. After the usual quickfire banter about Spurs, the Arsenal and Chelsea it was Tricks who made the first move.

'Frigging Dave is getting on my tits. I'm always happy to help Chris but I've never really liked old dog 'Smile -a-lot' and I don't trust him as far as I could throw him, which as you know is quite a long way. He seems to be in London every week and he keeps popping into the Gym to see me to ask his little favours. I'm giving Dave names of guys that do some very nasty things. We never did that before. Pup what the fuck is going on?'

'Why do you think Skip is ending his days in Malta? Do you know what a DDS is? Have you heard of Fancy Bear? What about the Internet of Things? That's 'what the fuck is going on?' guys!' said a smiling Pup with a chuckle in his voice.

'Jeez, Pup, you're not saying we're getting involved with the Russians, are you?' whispered Scalesy.

'Not necessarily, Scalesy, and we'll never know where the teams of hackers that Skip is using do come from. It's not espionage nor is it to use ransom ware nor is it disruption for its own sake. What Skip is doing is automating on a larger scale the kind of stuff he's been doing for years. It's his legacy.', Pup said quietly.

'But Dave is asking Tricks and I for more than information on the top ten lists, Pup. We figure explosives are going in the plumbing. This stuff is dangerous.' said Scalesy

'I think it'll soon be over, guys, as Skip hasn't got long to go and all the pieces in the jigsaw have to be in place before he goes. Then it'll just exist on the dark side of the web and we'll never know what's going on and neither will we be asked to do any more. The Chamberpots will be redundant. Stick with it, Skip won't harm us and he'll think it safest if none of us know the master plan. That includes Dave' said Pup, measuring his words so that Scalesy and Tricks knew he was confident in his explanation.

'Where does the IOT come in, Pup?' said Scalesy

'What the fuck is the IOT?' said Tricks

'Think of the IOT as all the smart devices connected to the internet such as mobiles, tablets, cameras, televisions, games consoles, robots, talking speakers you can ask questions of, sat navs, watches, fitness and health monitors – there's so many things. On most of these things the security is nothing like the same as computers.'

'And?' said Tricks

'The IOT will replace us by collecting data every day on thousands of targets. The CIA have been using smart televisions for years to listen in on their targets.'

'Where does Malta come into it? said Tricks

'Talent, easy access to countries and people useful to Skip, and above all, gaming and betting development, back offices and platforms.'

'And Dave?' said Tricks

'Think of him as the dealer in a game of blackjack. Skip sets up the people for Dave to meet in London and together they set up an electronic transfer to swap money, Skip's money, and the data. Only if they can make a deal, of course'.'

'So, you and Dave know the whole plan but the rest of us are taking the big risks but are still in the dark. You're not making me feel any fucking happier, Pup', said Tricks

'No, I don't think Pup or Dave will know the whole plan. Chris will think it safer if they don't know – am I right Pup? said Scalesy, maintaining eye contact with Tricks.

'Absolutely Scalesy. I'm sure that what I've guessed isn't the same as what Dave has guessed'.

'Will Trude or Steph know more than you and Dave? said Tricks

'I'm certain they won't, Trude is never mentioned and Steph is a civil servant, after all – they'll know nothing. Skip would never put us in danger and none of us would be where we are today without his contacts and backing. Look at me and all the corporate gigs I'm getting.'

'And we must keep taking orders from that prat, Smile-a-lot, do we?' said Tricks

'It won't be for long, Tricks, I'm sure and anyway Old Dog Dave has some useful contacts himself. For example, the famous and hot Charlene Wright, is joining you at the tennis– you lucky buggers' said Pup.

'So, you're not worried about Chris?' Scalesy said softly.

'Nope. I'm more worried about Dave. Discrete, he is not! He was bragging to me the other day about having lunch with Sir Angus Bottomley'

'What that government tosser the Met were after for kiddie sex?' interrupted Tricks

'That was just a rumour, Tricks, he's like our Warren Buffet – he does stuff for Government but he's still founder and chairman of an investment bank. He's a major player in fintech. He's very powerful.'

'How would Dave get to meet him, Pup, and why?' said Scalesy.

Pup shook his head. He could guess the answer to Scalesy's question but dare not let on.

6.

'Silly Sod' Dave muttered. Dave had just about got to the toilets at Kings Cross station in time. Very little leakage and that only caused by the 'ruddy idiots', men and women, that get all the way to the barrier before it dawns on them that they haven't got any change. Like rabbits stuck in headlights. This caused a queue of desperate, hopping mad people all trying to look cool. Dave was now comfortably seated and reading again the list of targets that were in Chris's handwritten letter.

Dave hated the mental effort of decoding Chris's instructions. Chris was obsessed by lists and numbers. Dave hated the effort and the insult to his intelligence. Dave never read Chris's articles and blogs. Dave hated looking back. Dave realised this last sentiment might be considered unusual by others that knew him as a retired history teacher and an avid collector of pre-1950 sports and variety theatre programmes. But to Dave what counted was right now. What interested him was what he'd do today and what would make tomorrow more fun. If it didn't make him happy or make him money – he wasn't interested.

'Bloody Holland & Barrett – I'll sue 'em', he thought, the thousands of pounds I've wasted on Saw Palmetto capsules. It's a passion killer too - always dashing to the loo, pinching your knob end …. That and piles … and skin folds … and a memory that splutters and sometimes flat lines …. and the falling ….and the anxiety … and the moods … the temper …but then again I look and act sharp … young for my age…about tomorrow not yesterday … not like Chris'.

It wasn't hard for Dave to remember the list but he needed to work out which of the Chamberpots could help Chris the most with each of them. There were only three new entries – all, unusually, American. Most of the names had been on the list for many years. Some, such as TB and SB, were publicly known to have their fingers in so many pies but had such powerful friends they were almost untouchable. Dave gave most thought to number 6, who he'd met. NM was Sir Nigel Morris, and he was the number one collectible. Dave's sister was married to Sir Nigel's brother.

Dave doubted whether the other Chamberpots would know NM. The niece that NM might be coming to see would be the ex-tennis star and socialite, Charlene Wright or Charlie as she was known to one and all. Charlie would be at the O2 tennis today, on Chris's instruction, as Uncle Dave's guest.

Sir Nigel Morris was a former Cabinet Secretary and almost certainly would know the 'what' and the 'who' of every cover up going; corporate crime, political corruption, regime change and what was behind media propaganda. He'd even know about assassinations – both character and person.

Chris's number one target is always number 6 on the list. This is a Chris joke which only fans of the late sixties. Prisoner' TV series would get. In the series, the Number 2 would act as the Head of the Village of prisoners – like a President of any state in the world. The burning question was 'Who is Number 1?'

The main character, the Prisoner, was played by Patrick McGoohan, who also wrote and directed the most important episodes. He was Number 6. In 'Fall Out', the last episode, Number 6 gets to see Number 1 who looks uncannily like himself. Dave was as much a fan of the series as Chris, but for totally different reasons.

Number 10 on the list is always FST. This refers to the late, Frederick Seward Trueman, who gives legitimacy to the list being about 'Sporting Greats'. About the only thing Dave agreed with Chris on was that FST was the 'greatest bloody fast bowler that ever drew breath'. This was FST's description of himself. Fiery Fred Trueman was a fellow Yorkshireman. He was a superstar cricketer in the late fifties and sixties. When Chris and Dave were at school together FST was their sporting hero.

Dave tore up this last page of Chris's letter with the list on it. He flushed the small shreds down the toilet. Outside, he washed his hands and looked in the mirror.

For a decade or more he'd always been surprised at how very pale and smooth his skin was. He wished he had enough hair to be worth combing. He thought the upper half of his head looked just like many of the free-range eggs he collected weekly from his cousin's farm in Cloughton.

The clues to his sixty-eight years were the grey hair surrounding his shiny, bald pate, the brown marks on his cheeks and neck, the deep wrinkles in the forehead and an open fan of, what seemed like, fine cuts at the side of his eyes. The dark semi circles under his eyes he'd had for as long as he could remember. 'Born like that, maybe?' He felt he looked quite hard and fit still. Certainly, he looked hard enough for any young lout to think twice about picking on him. 'Damn' - I should have trimmed my nose and ears - typical – not a hair seen for years up top but it sprouts everywhere else like crazy'.

He smiled at the mirror. The mirror replied with a one careful owner, full set of, slightly off white, teeth. Despite, hundreds of attempts, and chewing so much gum he could fart for England, he'd never fully kicked the fags. He knew it was a winning smile – a smile which he hoped was still on a lucky streak. He liked turning it on. He smiled again, straightened his tie and silently mouthed to the mirror 'Show Time'.

Dave knew he'd be the only one in a blazer and tie. They'd expect him to be the 'life and soul' of the O2 get together, but his heart wasn't really in it. Chris's current crusade probably involved all of them, to some degree, but Dave would be the only one who knew just how dangerous the people were whom Chris had instructed him to meet. Dave wouldn't be sorry when it was over and 'Skip' was dead. This couldn't come soon enough.

Dave had never called Chris, 'Skip'. His hatred of his schoolfriend increased when Chris was voted captain of their cricket team rather than himself. He'd be pleased with closure soon on thirty years of an itch he needed to scratch. He consoled himself that he could look forward to the journey back to York with Charlie.

CHAPTER THREE: The Lord Chamberlain's Men

Group: several people sharing something in common

1.

'I SLEEP BEST AFTER SEX but even then, I'm just not sleeping nowadays', said Dave.

'It'll be your waterworks?' suggested Trude, in a loud stage whisper.

'Not after sex… main thing on my mind is whether I might get another go later and if my little mate will be up for the job!' said Dave, even more loudly.

'You wish. Dream on, Dave' said Tricks quietly.

'God, you must be talking about a bloody long time ago, Dave. Are you, or are you not, up and down to the loo all night - like the rest of us?' added Scalesy, laughing,

Steph, looked down to the other end of their row of seats, 'in the Gods', to where Dave, at the end of the row, had lit the blue touch paper on another topic upon which Scalesy, Tricks and Trude were building the quick-fire banter. Steph was next to Trude and Dave's guest Charlie, was at the other end of the row. Along with the very many spectators in earshot Steph and Charlie were the audience for the four Chamberpots in their presence. 'Chamberpots' was Trude's nickname for the Lord Chamberlain's Men - the name Chris gave the founder members around thirty years ago.

Steph could see the day was beginning to go well. The laughter, snorts, tears, and the 'shushing' from those around them with a humour bypass, were all on the increase. Steph felt, as always, lucky to be in their company. She was there as the absent Chris's guest. Over the last fifteen years she'd attended many of the Chamberpots' days out.

These get-togethers usually entailed watching big sports events. They'd been many times to see football, rugby and cricket matches but this was only their second time to watch tennis.

Once, Tricks had taken them to see Summer Slam wrestling at Wembley Stadium. Steph didn't class wrestling as a sport but she surprised herself by really enjoying the entertainment. However, Steph's three favourite days had been non-sporting ones and all had been at the theatre. Chris got a box for them all to see Julian Clary as Emcee in 'Cabaret'. The final scene where the cast was naked awaiting to go into the gas chamber would never leave Steph's memory bank.

Pup had arranged for them to see the amazing Penn and Teller in a rare London gig and then Scalesy had got tickets for the ten thousandth performance of Phantom of the Opera. Andrew Lloyd Webber and Michael Crawford came onto the stage at the end and spoke to the audience. On all three occasions Steph felt it had been a total privilege to be in the audience.

It was Charlie's first time at a Chamberpots get together and Steph was trying to make sure that Charlie wasn't intimidated by this irresolute bunch of old fogeys or bothered by audience members that recognised her. Steph knew Charlie was an ex-tennis pro and that she was eagerly looking forward to the singles match. They'd already seen a doubles match in which the Bryan twins had won and treated the crowd to their celebratory, airborne chest bumps.

Despite the smiles and giggles, Steph was conscious of how stiffly she was holding her neck and back and that made her feel as though she was sitting under a huge spotlight that shone down on her declaring that she wasn't yet into this visit to the O2 arena to see the ATP Finals. It was partly that she wasn't too bothered about the tennis action, it wasn't one of her favourite sports. Mainly, though it was that she knew everyone was worried about what Chris might be up to and so another kind of virtual spotlight would be on her later.

She drifted back to it. Scalesy had spotted a bit in the paper and was reading it out loud to the others:

'Out of a poll of six thousand holidaymakers, ten per cent of men, but only four per cent of women had sex on a plane'.

Dave picked up the cue and with a flourish, hand shielding mouth, smiled and then stage whispered:

'So how does that work then?'

The comments came thick and fast:

'Must have been an abundance of gay male airline stewards';

'Is abundance the right collective noun for a group of gay male stewards?'

'Does sex include masturbation?'

'Does oral sex only count as sex for one party? Clinton said it wasn't even sex!'

'Surely it's a 'fling' or a 'flight' or a 'rash' or even a 'thong' of gay stewards?'

'Did you know some amazing things happen to bodily fluids at altitude?'

Tricks was the quiet one of the four Chamberpots. Steph hadn't seen him for a few years and she was astonished at just how glam and big he looked. It was lucky that Scalesy's guest hadn't been able to come because Tricks needed the empty seat to spread his muscled bulk over. He was wearing dark glasses, presumably those that you can see through in all light, and a very expensive black, silk suit. Steph guessed that it was Armani. His white, silk shirt was open at the collar and Steph was certain that he had a Rolex. He'd made a big effort to outshine his mates today. He had shoulder length, bleach blonde hair and was very, very big – must be seventeen maybe eighteen stone. But it wasn't fat, Tricks was clearly pumped up. Steph wondered where Tricks had got the money to dress like that. She had a habit of forensically evaluating everything about a person and that included what they chose to wear.

Steph was beginning to find the noise irritating. The Chamberpots seemed to be all shouting at once and the arena was very noisy. She closed her eyes briefly and immediately an image of Chris appeared behind her eyelids. She felt an unexpected pang of longing for him. It took her but surprise, especially since she had had not had that kind of feeling for many years, their relationship now something that would be placed in the 'comfortable old shoe' category. She shrugged slightly her eyes till closed, enjoying the reverie, that was doing a good job of blocking out the hubbub.

The noise was trying, and, now she thought about it, it had surprised her the previous time too. Naively, she'd expected a predominance of white and green but the court and surrounds were blue. No one wore white. They felt like a mile away from the action and were mostly watching the cube of big screens rather than the tiny blue court below them.

'Hey, you ok?' It was Tricks. Steph blinked her eyes open.

'Yes, I'm fine, thanks.'

The crowd didn't behave like the crowds that Steph had seen on television at Wimbledon. There were quiet, gasps of excitement mainly, during the points but they were screamingly loud at all other times. The O2 arena was massive. It was a cacophony of shouts, lasers, and multiple images on the big screens, bass driven rock and evangelical announcements. Steph thought that it would be the worst kind of environment for an epileptic, she wondered if any ever did attend?

Steph was gripping her programme far too tightly. Relax. It wasn't going to happen. There would be no potential conflict of loyalty between job and country against her good friend and lover. Or was it ex-lover? Chris was against many individuals within the establishment but he was never pro violence. He'd been seething for years but Steph knew he was no terrorist. It would involve technology, for sure. He'd talked about Smart City and the i-gaming sector in Malta. Still she wasn't sure how far his anger and illness might take him.

Last time they'd seen Robin Soderling and Rafael Nadal in the singles and this year it was Nadal and the Frenchman, Jo Wilfried Tsonga. They were out on the blue court now and had finished knocking up. Steph thought Nadal looked all muscly cuteness, in his all black kit, with lime trims, but small in comparison with Tsonga. Trude, whose get-together this was, and who was very much into tennis as both an ex-player and a regular spectator had said that Tsonga had a reputation for blinding but erratic power – he was a gambler. Steph thought he might be a pussycat off the court and he had a wonderful smile to go along with his brutal serve. Charlie said 'That was nothing – you should see Djoko, Roddick and Berdych's serves'. Steph had never heard of Djoko, Roddick or Berdych.

Steph checked her programme and read that there was only three inches difference in height between the gladiators – six feet one inch as against six feet four inches. She assumed there would be differences in lifestyle between them though. Call it female intuition but there must be. She'd seen that Nadal, despite being World Number 2, still lives in the town of his birthplace in Mallorca, and his coach had always been his Uncle Toni.

The early exchanges of the match confirmed that these two, like most top professionals, were 'in the zone' and very serious about it all. Certainly, the players smiling at or chatting to the crowd was as likely as Tricks stopping his annoying shouts of 'C'mon Rafa'.

Rafa looked gorgeous but Jo looked fun and was the underdog. Steph decided against the World Number 2 and Tricks' choice.

'C'mon Jo', she shouted in unison with Tricks' 'C'mon Rafa'.

2.

After the tennis, Trude had booked a plain, but friendly looking Greek restaurant to have a quick meal in. Steph was relieved. After the noise and bustle of the O2 complex, the cramming and shoving on the tube, at last, here in the restaurant, she might relax. It was her kind of place. It would have looked the same fifty years ago. It had white tablecloths, cutlery laid, and olive oil and vinegar bottles. The Greek owners' family probably undertook most of the jobs here. Their waiter looked as if he'd been here forever. It felt like a family mealtime. For a moment, the ghost of the pang of regret she had felt earlier twisted itself in her stomach, but she took the menu being proffered by Trude and studied it till the feeling went away.

The restaurant was ideally located, within walking distance of Russell Square, Euston, St Pancras and Kings Cross stations. After the meal, they'd all be making their various train journeys back home. Steph didn't mention it but this was close to where the bus had blown up on 7/7.

Steph knew that Chris had heard the explosion at the Night 'n Day café just up the road. He'd got caught up in what he called 'the Bermuda triangle' of explosions as he'd walked from Kings Cross underground, after that was cordoned off, to Russell Square. He'd quickly appreciated he was in the middle of a major incident. The shocked, soot covered, walking wounded hurrying away from the scene was a definite give-away that this was a major incident. He could do nothing useful and so he decided to stay put with a cappuccino. The television in the café said the underground closures and explosions were due to power surges. Then he heard the explosion. The top deck of the bus and the people on it were blown away.

Many hours later, when he'd been able to get a mobile signal and a pint, in a hotel – all the shops and pubs were shut down – he'd rung Steph. He said he felt useless, hopeless, helpless, bitter and overwhelmingly sad. He had pride for all the heroes of that day – the firemen, doctors, nurses, police, tube staff, ordinary citizens in the way they'd all put others first. Chris was raging. He seemed as angry with government officials as he was with the terrorists. The rage never left him.

He raged about Blair and Bush, the Carlyle Group, Cheney and News International. He raged about the media blackout. He'd shouted at Steph that 'it was like Fox News and Iraq but now 'in our own fucking country'. He'd told her to tell her bosses that there are 'no bloody oil wells' to protect in the London underground'

Most people would think Chris was a thinker not a doer. Steph knew differently and she knew he had a temper. Only his temper would have made him use his mobile and rage at a civil servant, even if she was his lover, on such a day. On 7/7 2005 Steph was the outlet for his rage. She was also rather pleased to be the only person he'd chosen to ring that day. Steph felt again as though Chris's spirit had crossed the ocean and was trailing them that day, and who knows? Maybe it had.

3.

In the restaurant Steph was seated between Trude and Dave. Opposite her was Scalesy who was flanked by Charlie and Tricks. Steph always tried to sit next to Trude. She liked Trude a lot. Trude called a spade a spade. Sitting next to Trude also helped Steph's self-confidence. Steph was no delicate creature herself but Trude was much larger.

Steph dressed well in comparison with Trude too. Trude, like Pat, her mother, always seemed to wear clothes one size too small. They both looked as though they'd chosen their wardrobe from the best of the charity shops. They hadn't but it was 'sensible' clothing rather than fashionable. Steph thought that Trude's fleece, blouse and jeans made Steph's jacket and trousers, from the Per Una range at Marks and Spencer's, look sensational. Sat next to Trude, Steph felt able to cope with the designer clad, stick insect that was Charlie.

Trude was oblivious to what she looked like. There had been a time when she was almost completely obsessed with how she had looked – she had to be. When she was young she looked good in everything and prided herself that, with the right motivation, she could get back to nearly the same size as she was then.

Almost as soon as they got into the restaurant Charlie started interrogating them about the Chamberpots. Charlie found out first that 'Chamberpots' was Trude's irreverent abbreviation for 'The Lord Chamberlain's Men'. Chris had given the founding group this name in 1984. Chris had told them that although all eight, would be equal shareholders, in what was an invisible company, he was going to be, the William Shakespeare, the leader of 'The Men'. The eight were Trude, Scalesy, Tricks, Dave, Geoff, Pup – Geoff's son, Nick and Chris.

Chris, as Shakespeare, would be the head writer, actor and director. In Chris's words, they would be 'actors one and all and all for one and I'm the one and then all's well that ends well'. It was all complete rubbish. It was an excuse for the eight of them to arrange to meet up a few times each year. Later it became an excuse for them all, when asked, to provide Chris with information to help him hasten the resignations of some of the hypocrites governing the nation and major institutions.

The group had first come together in 1984 at the Station Hotel, an erstwhile pub in Easingwold, North Yorkshire. This was during a cricket tour to Yorkshire of the Middlesex University Invaders (Wandering) Cricket Club. Chris was captain. Of the original eight in the Lord Chamberlain's Men, five of them were Londoners and three; Chris, Trude and Dave, were from Yorkshire and lived in London. Chris lived in London from the age of eighteen and never returned to his roots whereas Trude and Dave did.

Dave and Chris were both Beverley Grammar School Old Boys. They were the same age and both took their first degrees at Middlesex Polytechnic in London. That they ended up at the same university, albeit at different campuses and studying different subjects, was just a coincidence. But they did join the same sports teams. Trude, a friend of Chris's, was the only female Chamberpot. Trude, although not a part of the 1984 cricket tour, had been in Yorkshire at her parents and joined the tourists for a couple of their post-match revelries. Matt (Tricks), Ricky (Scalesy), Nick, Pup (Steve) and Geoff were all in the Invaders cricket team, with Dave and Chris.

Steve (Pup) was very young when on this tour which is why he was given the nickname 'Pup'. Geoff, Pup's father, died in the late nineties. Geoff would always be celebrated as the creator of the Chamber Pots signature handshake.

The Chamberpots have a special greeting, to each other, in as public a place as possible. It involves walking towards the other with two fingers, like a pair of scissors, outstretched. As their fingers are about to entwine, they raise them, to eye level, shouting simultaneously 'FUCK OFF'. They then turn around immediately, back to back, with the two fingers now as a gun, close to their chest, pointing upwards, as if they are about to start a duel. Then both lean forward and bump each other's bums.

This is done with great speed to ensure it is a shock to any audience that may have assembled. It rarely fails to gain applause. Steph noticed that Charlie was the only one in the restaurant that didn't applaud when Scalesy and Dave demonstrated it.

A new fact about Geoff, who Steph never met, emerged in this latest rendition of the history of the Chamber Pots. Apparently, Chris and Scalesy had almost spontaneously combusted at Geoff's funeral. They found out then that the creator of their silly handshake was not only well known to the vicar as a regular church goer, but was also a founder member and high ranking Grand Master of a Freemason's Lodge. Naturally, Geoff, a leading light in North London's Accountancy profession, had kept all the above quiet from his fellow Lord Chamberlain's Men.

None of this was really answering Charlie's question, which was 'So what do the Chamberpots do? Steph, after the mezes were finished, along with the first bottles of house red and white, tried to move things on by asking the question again.

'Why don't you guys say what you decided to do together?' Steph teased.

Charlie said 'Yes, do tell. Like Dave just said, a few times a year you do a get together at a major event but that's not all you do, is it?' Her eyes were bright and hungry for detail, she reminded Steph of one of those news hounds who follow people who have been involved in scandals, trying to get them to talk.

'Excellent Dave – thanks for inviting a journalist into our midst. That's a first' said Tricks sarcastically and quietly, but he continued

'Well, it all started the morning after the heavy night before. The night Scalesy was given his name'.

Tricks grinned, looked across to Scalesy and said

'Tell Charlie why we call you Scalesy – and it's nothing to do with Scholesy of Man U?'

'Gawd - do I have to?' Scalesy said in mock protest

'All for one' yelled Tricks, Dave and Trude in unison.

'Well, if you insist. It's like this Charlie. My true friends, work colleagues and family call me Ricky, except for my mother who calls me Richard. However, since August 1984 this rabble will only call me Scalesy. I guess I'm luckier than a middle-aged man still being called Pup'.

Scalesy took a deep breath, checked his audience were alert and started;

'It may have been the cumulative effect of the four previous days and nights drinking, with, no sleep. Whatever, it was poor judgment on my part. This lot never gives anyone an even break and they certainly don't forget anything embarrassing. Not for them 'What happens in Vegas stays in Vegas'. For them it's more like 'Whatever happens on tour will be reported and used in evidence against you, every time we bloody well get together.'

Steph liked Scalesy. He was what her mother would have called dapper. He was the smallest of the Chamber Pots and was always dressed neatly. He was very gentle, intelligent, good mannered and precise in everything he did and that was reflected in his appearance. Short dark hair, square features, clear green eyes, clean shaven, rimless glasses, dark jeans, polished black brogues and an expensive white and blue Crew sweat shirt, with a red T shirt underneath it. He owned his own plumbing business which had a very wealthy clientele. Chris had referred many of these. Scalesy joked that he was 'a man with five vans'. He was successful. Steph liked him so much that she was even happy re-hearing his story for the umpteenth time. She had noticed something about herself as she was getting older. Sometimes she was happy to listen to someone repeat themselves or waffle about nothing almost in the spirit of 'hitching a free ride' letting her mind wander as they chattered, confident that she could take those few moments to drift and keep up. As a young woman she would have despised this kind of verbiage, and cut in to end the ramble. It was a curious thing, really, her apparent greater tolerance.

Scalesy continued: 'I'd been explaining to Trude why men and women were so badly designed to participate in most Olympic events. I won't digress into our actual discussions about what constitutes a true Olympic sport. But, I will just say that anything with a racket, ball, oar or a horse most definitely isn't. At the London Olympics, I will be going to many events, courtesy of Chris, to adjudicate on their legitimacy.

I digress. Trude and I agreed that the human body is not fit for purpose in Olympic sports. Tits, balls and prick – or the latter's cumulative word – 'tackle' – are significant impediments to true Olympic sporting achievement. At that point Tricks, and we'll explain how Tricks came by his name on another occasion, … ahem, … for it is Tricks who I blame for these events, said something like 'But women, even the lovely small breasted species and definitely those with tits like Trude's – effing exhibition class - are surely impeded more than men. Their top bits are much heavier than men's lower bits'.

Scalesy paused for effect and to sip some water. He continued, 'You'll have gathered that this was a highly technical discussion on male and female anatomy. Old dog Dave, the scheming little sod, then seized upon Tricks' interesting theory of relativity. Dave shouted, something like, 'I'll bet five pints that tackle is heavier than tits'. I responded 'Right then, we'd better have them weighed. Come on Trude'.

Then, followed by the ever gorgeous Trude, Tricks, Dave, Chris, Nick, Geoff, and Pup and, at a conservative estimate, twenty others, I led the way to the kitchen. There I found some scales. I'd just put my tackle into the receptacle when the new landlord of the Station Hotel, who hadn't really entered the spirit of our stay in his establishment, walked in. He said something that sounded like. - I say, 'sounded like', because I think your hearing is somewhat impaired when you've got your tackle on the scales. It sounded like 'what the fuck are you doing – you're a dirty little bastard!' So, from that day forth I've been known as Scalesy.'

'Thanks for that Scalesy' said Tricks, 'anyway that tour was a real eye-opener and not just for seeing Scalesy's tackle weighed. It was the time of the Miners' strike and just talking to the lads that lived there, and their wives and girlfriends, shocked us all. We just weren't in the know, at all, in London. In fact, the rioting around Fitzwilliam, that had started six weeks or so before, was nothing in comparison with what had been happening day to day to the strikers and their families and ….'

Trude interrupted Tricks.

'Charlie, you've got to understand this really was a big deal then. My parents were in the thick of it in Donny at the time. I certainly got riled a few times about what them southern softies thought was going off against what was really going off. Thatcher was starving kids to make their parents give in. In fact, you Dave', Trude pointed at Dave; 'riled me the most saying that you didn't think pickets and striking was the right option. It was the ONLY option.' Trude's nostrils were slightly flared now as she warmed to her topic. Charlie thought that she looked like a slightly aging Boudicca. She had what they used to call 'an indomitable air.'

'Do you remember when that lad said the police beating up miners, on the picket lines, was just routine – he said it was 'bobbies enjoying their sen'. Phone tapping, curfews, trumped up prosecutions and delayed trials. Hell, it was like a military coup'

Tricks came back in 'Thatcher's government was so serious about forcibly quelling protests and destroying the miners' morale that they deployed a national police force. They were bussing as many as two thousand police from picket line to picket line. They were armed to the teeth - helmets, shields, batons and horses. The nearest thing we've had to it since was Acid House and shutting down all the massive raves. Today, NATO would be involved and telling Thatcher that they'd have to intervene by bombing the House of Commons and Buckingham Palace, as command and control centres, to protect innocent citizens – NOT.

If the scenes were televised today of the police putting down the unarmed pickets these scenes would stand up as just as bad as anything happening to unarmed protesters in the Middle East and North Africa. Anyway, it led inevitably to the Battle of Orgreave. They sent eight thousand police to inflict serious damage on five thousand pickets. It was a government planned war against union power and the first step was closing down the mines and the miners' livelihoods.'

Charlie was getting impatient. After all, 1984 was a long time ago. Charlie remembered the name Arthur Scargill and that one of her uncles had said he'd lost it when he started doing Hitler type rallies but that was about it. So, she interrupted Tricks; 'What's this got to do with the Chamberpots. I still don't know what you do?'

A smiling Dave came in at this point. He knew that neither Tricks nor Trude would take well to being interrupted. 'The Chamberpots, as we now call them weren't really formed that last day of the tour but the group of eight of us, now the secret seven, had got on really well. Chris sensed we all wanted to do something about the injustices to the miners. He wanted to do something about redressing the government and the media propaganda. Hell, they even tried to make out that Scargill, the Miners' leader, was mad and fashioning himself after Hitler. You know the score – just like they did with Saddam, Gadaffi and Assad.'

Tricks picked up the baton and continued 'Over the last few weeks of the cricket season, back in London, Chris kept saying to us we should do something to help. Then when we were playing our six a side, end of season competition, he told us what he was going to do. Chris had a top job in HR for a big multinational – him and Dave were older than the rest of us and I suppose we looked up to them a bit, not that we would now.'.

'You never looked up to me, surely? It's always been follow my leader – mainly because he could flash the cash - anyway, carry on Tricks' smiled Dave.

'So, when Chris said something we usually listened. He said he was going to do something to help the miners and would we help him? His plan was that as the Lord Chamberlains Men we'd get together a few times a year. Each of us would take it in turn to choose an event we'd go to – that way we could chat together about anything we wanted to do. We'd never have to put anything in writing or use phones and so on. He'd be the one that would find a way to expose the 'hypocrites', the truth underneath the propaganda. We'd just help him get the information that would lead to their exposure and if we got lucky they may even resign and …'

'I've got it' interrupted Dave, laughing, 'The key word is 'exposing'. I now know why Chris has scarpered to Malta. It's to do more exposing. He's a secret flasher, a sex tourist and he's probably doing a Gary Glitter'.

They all laughed, apart from Steph. Steph was fiddling with her cutlery. She said quietly:

'He may have just gone there to die.' Steph looked around the room. That shut them up. She would normally have used this kind of conversation stopper for effect but she realised that the thought of Chris dying was forming a lump in her throat. 'Carry on Tricks' she said.

'OK. That's about it really. Each of us would do the best they could to get Chris information he needed. The first thing he did was to persuade a company that provided him with management training videos to allow some independent filmmakers to use their studios. There were these guys who had footage of what was really happening to the miners. Chris sorted it so they could turn their footage into films. The rest of us helped find out who might distribute and play the films. So that was the start of it. Any questions, class?'.

Charlie had been drifting in and out of this lengthy monologue by Tricks. She did remember that in 1984 she was a toddler and had been given her first mini tennis racket. She hated it. It made her hands sore. Her mother would say 'Hit it harder Charlene. Hit it harder' and eventually she'd throw a tantrum and the racket, sometimes at her mother. She wished she hadn't started this discussion with the Chamberpots. She could sense tension about the absent Chris. But she decided to ask one more question 'So what have you all done since these films, then?

'Well, I suppose the answer is that we don't really know. Only Chris knows. Of course, we remember all our brilliant get-togethers. Each of us knows any information we've given to Chris. From time to time we might spot disclosures, letters, articles, blogs and even news stories that Chris might have prompted. But only Chris will know what he's achieved and he's not going to start telling people, including us. He's happy, and we're happy for him, to stay under the radar' said Trude

'Sometimes I see something, like a good bit of investigative reporting, about bribes or expenses or dodgy government contracts which leads to someone resigning. If it's someone I know Chris would want to resign then I'll suspect his hand in it. We know that he takes information we've provided and gives it to freelance journalists, who he funds to do the story. He's not short of a bob or two and he's always said that good investigative journalism needs funding by people like him because the mainstream media won't do it. But like Trude says I never know for sure and I guess I know him better than anyone here. He's not doing anything more than a PR agency would do and certainly he's doing nothing wrong ', added, the ever smiling, Dave.

Steph noticed that after Dave said this and someone else started talking he took a pen out of his inside pocket and wrote on a paper napkin the word 'Spoons'. He then put the napkin and pen in his inside pocket.

'So, where do I come in?' said Charlie.

'Dave said that you might be a bit of a handful. Look Charlie, don't make us out to be something we're not – we're just a group of old friends. The get-togethers are the important thing. We take it in turns to organise them. The organiser, like Trude is today, buys seven tickets. If any of us can't make it then we invite guests to take up the places – like you and Steph. Is that okay with you?' Said Scalesy, quietly and firmly.

Steph could see that Charlie had realised that, even the very affable, Scalesy was looking to close this conversation. Charlie was also the sort of person that didn't mind seeing how far she could push it. Charlie turned to Steph and said:

'Do you think you're here just to watch some tennis?'

'Absolutely', said Steph. 'They're sports mad'

'Okay', said Charlie, deciding to stop scratching at open wounds. Charlie had really enjoyed Jo's win. She could see why Steph liked to be invited to the Chamberpots meet ups and she'd like to be on the reserve list in future. She didn't want to embarrass her Uncle Dave either. So, smooth as silk, she just changed the subject:

'I think I've got all that – do you think those hunky top pros are told by the ATP that they've got to change their shirts every set, just so that we girls get a cheap thrill?'

'I just hope the match wasn't fixed', said Trude.

4.

Pup realised he'd stopped sweating. His face was drying up. His back, armpits, forearms and calves would remain wet until the end of his act. But it was all OK now. They're mine. I'm on cruise control. Pup's smile became genuine. In front of him, inside the Grand Connaught Rooms, he could see the crossed arms were unfolding. He could see teeth. Heads were shaking and flopping back in laughter. There was that special buzz. The few seconds of incredulity, followed by the whispers of 'How did he do that?' and then followed by the applause.

Pup started sweating the moment he put his dress shirt on. He delayed putting it on as long as possible and kept the dressing room, when he was given one, as cool as possible. No matter what he did to stay cool, he would be pouring sweat by the time he came on stage. He'd carry on sweating until the moment when the audience was his. It had just happened and tonight he was only five minutes into his act.

Pup gazed at his stage partner and said 'OK then. Say: Peter Piper pecked a peck of pickled pepper. A peck of pickled pepper Peter Piper pecked'.

'Shan't' said Stormy

'OK. Let's see. Say: Bring me a bottle of beer and brown bread and butter'

'Ruck Off' said Stormy, the pool player, swinging his cue and wooden head to face the audience and raising his thick, black wool eyebrows.

'Stormy you've got to show these nice people your talent'

'Show 'em yours first, sunshine'

'How about: She sells seashells on the sea shore.' said Pup

'Sod sea shells she sells on the sea shore – how much more of this shit have you got?' said Stormy

Laughter fills the room. Pup shrugged and gave a 'What can I do with him' look to the audience. A thought came to him. He knew what Chris's cuttings on fireworks and frame-ups meant. Chris wanted Pup's help with a series of illusions.

'As much or as little of this shit as that nice Mr. Williams, over there, wants' said Pup

ACT TWO: APRIL 2012

CHAPTER FOUR: Backstage Nerves

Coincidence: A chance concurrence, happenstance or twist of fate.

1.

SIR NIGEL MORRIS WAS BEGINNING to feel his age. He was already convinced that sixty-two was an old age. This was despite his wife, daughter and even his niece, Charlie, trying to assure him that seventy was the new fifty. Sir Nigel certainly wouldn't fit the archetypal image of a retired senior civil servant. For a start, he wasn't stooped and there wasn't a grey hair on his head. He had a full head of mousey coloured hair and was an upright, but slim and muscular, six-footer. He was very fit and swam every morning at his London club. He also ran marathons when the security allowed.

His back and head hurt this morning, but that was caused by nothing more sinister than the hotel bed. The Royal York hotel, adjacent to York railway station, was convenient and it had beautifully furnished bedroom suites with all the refreshments you may require. Nevertheless, Sir Nigel would just mention to the Hotel manager that it was important that they improved the quality of the double beds.

Fortunately, it was a one-night stay and he would be back in London by early afternoon. He had three meetings in the hotel that morning and the last one he was looking forward to most of all, because that was with his favourite niece, Charlie. He thought to himself how refreshing it was not to have to tear around from place to place making speeches. When he'd been Cabinet Secretary and Permanent Secretary of the Cabinet Office, he was also effectively head of the Civil Service. This meant that wherever he travelled there was likely to be some Civil Service office where the 'troops' required a morale boosting visit and speech from him. Not that Sir Nigel had ever been complimented on his ability to make motivational speeches. Thoughtful, intelligent and ruthless were the adjectives most applied to Sir Nigel's demeanour.

Charlene's father, his brother, had been a silly man. Like Sir Nigel he'd been well educated, Oxford, and he'd had a very successful career as a dentist, a dentist to the stars on many occasions. However, none of this had stopped him from being a silly man.

Sir Nigel had never thought of his brother as a particularly brave man either. So, it was a surprise some six years ago when his brother, James, had left his wife and family to live in Australia with a much younger male anaesthetist. It was even more surprising to Sir Nigel that someone who wore purple shirts could have hidden his plans so well about escaping Britain. He'd also done well to hide the fact, for so long, that he was gay, especially as so many family members had always suspected he was.

Sir Nigel had promised his sister in law that the next time he was 'Oop North' he would make sure that he saw his niece, Charlie. This was a pleasure. Charlie had all the languid, lean, tall, athletic, good looks and manner of her mother. Sir Nigel knew that Charlie was ambitious and wanted to achieve a great deal in the world of sports media and marketing, and certainly his contact network could be of value to her ambition.

Sir Nigel had been in Commerce early in his career that had made him attractive to the Treasury, which then led to him becoming Press Secretary to the Chancellor and finally to be appointed Cabinet Secretary. Even then he'd represented the UK on the IMF and nowadays had many Non-Executive Directorships. He was currently Chair of the finance committees of two of Britain's greatest sporting institutions. He could, and would happily, be useful to Charlie.

Sir Nigel had always acknowledged that women were not appreciative subjects of either his wit or his wisdom. He wasn't expecting an easy ride from his somewhat fiery niece. He'd pretty much got out of the firing line by the time Condoleesa Rice and Hillary Clinton became regular visitors of the PMs, but he could imagine that Charlie in 20 years' time would have their similar, and fearful to many, presence. Thatcher could be frightening in her conviction too, but, surprisingly to those who did not know her, her feminine wiles seemed to soften the blow.

There was a delicate matter that would require some of his famed tact and diplomacy. His sister-in-law had made it clear that she wanted Sir Nigel to convey to Charlie that she needed to do something about her relationship with her husband.

The Morris family did not like it that Charlie's husband, of only a few years, lived so publicly far apart from Charlie. This would be fine if they were in different countries, work commitments could be the excuse. In the same country being two hundred miles away from your husband, who didn't appear to have any intention of working, made it a very public separation. He would tell Charlie to get back to London and pretend to reconcile before divorcing him. Sir Nigel's wife couldn't give a damn about Charlie's marriage, but she really would not tolerate them making it so easy for the press to create news by gossip and the constant stream of photographs of Charlie and her husband's new partners.

Sir Nigel agreed that it was not a good idea for the Morris family to be in the public eye so regularly. The Chilcot Inquiry into the rationale for the Iraq war had dragged Sir Nigel back into the public eye briefly but that would soon be forgotten. If Charlie and her husband could be divorced quickly then much of the gossip about Charlie, her husband, her father and her Uncle would stop. So, he had some contacts that could help Charlie and Charlie could help him by divorcing her husband. This would be a classic win-win negotiation. Sir Nigel enjoyed negotiating.

2.

Charlie went through the swing doors of the Royal York hotel and walked down the long corridor towards reception. About halfway down this corridor Charlie saw, or at least she thought she saw, in the distance walking from left to right, her Uncle Dave. Charlie quickened her step, turned right at reception and fully expected to see Dave in the cafe bar, but there was no sign of him.

She walked outside onto the balcony of the cafe bar, which gave her a full view of people walking into the station and walking away from the station into York. Dave was nowhere to be seen. She texted him

'Just saw you – same hotel. Where u go?' Almost immediately the reply came back 'Not me - home in Scarborough'.

A small frown creased Charlie's forehead but with a shrug of her shoulders she pocketed her phone and looked around her. Her statuesque figure always drew glances from men as well as women and she allowed herself a small smile as she clocked a man easily 10 years younger than her looking her over. The shrug of her shoulder had given her a twinge of pain and she rotated it gingerly. It was a constant reminder of a career in tennis that she could have had. The fact that she had, in one slip crashed to the ground and out of any chance of a professional tennis career ate her up and she used to wake up at night sweating and in tears of frustration at what she had lost. Charlie had loved the adoration, the expectation, the victory and the pride that people had shown in her.

It had started at boarding school where her long legs and strong forearm had her winning everything for the school and eventually the county. Big fish, small pond. But when she left, the success continued until one day, playing on grass, she had slipped and landed on her shoulder. The arm that had once swung so powerfully now could barely be raised above the elbow.

After a period of mourning for her tennis career lost, Charlie had picked herself up and dusted herself off and was now admired for thinking on her feet, the 'go to girl' if an inventive solution was needed or a problem proved particularly intractable.

It was a trade-off, a poor one she sometimes thought, but satisfactory. Charlie had realized that she needed to be the best at something, and if that was as a 'smart cookie' then that would have to do, that and the admiration for her tall striking looks. Charlie recognized that she needed that, and she got it.

3.

Tricks overheard his business partner, Spit, demonstrating his life-long belief that the customer is always wrong:

'Nah you can't have a year's membership. Tell you what. I'll give you a deal on six weeks. Doubt if you'll last that long but if you do we can talk about extending it.'

The customer was a forty something father of irritable twins, with ice cream covered noses and mouths. He was leant on the reception desk looking at the price list. Meanwhile the twins, in the double pushchair next to their father, were throwing toys at each other. The father picked up a green elephant and purple Martian off the floor, threw them back in the pushchair, said 'I'll think about it' and walked out.

'Ding, ding. Another sale made by the Peak Fitness top salesman of the year' said Tricks with a big grin. Tricks was standing just inside the entrance to the gym. He was spotting for a heavily tattooed gorilla that was bench-pressing 180kg.

Spit was named after a TV comedian-come-ventriloquist's dummy. Spit the dog only made one sound - the sound of clearing his throat, ready to spit. Spit didn't turn around to look at Tricks but stared through the open door, cleared his throat and slowly croaked:

'Fuck me. Today is our lucky day - one timewaster out and another in. Here's your young magician friend – ask him if he knows how to make my missus disappear'.

'Hi Spit, Hi Tricks', Pup said walking through towards Tricks and the gorilla. Only Pup called him 'Tricks' in his gym and no-one called him by his real name, Matt. To everyone in the gym, for as long as any of them could remember, Tricks was Ric – a look-alike for the American wrestler and superstar Ric Flair. To Pup he was Tricks because of his bar diving exploits and drinking challenges on cricket tours and Chamberpots get-togethers.

Pup and Tricks, lived in Hendon. The gym was just off Brent Street, behind the Tesco supermarket. Pup dropped by, now and again, on his way to Hendon Central tube station. Tricks and Pup knew a lot of the same people in the London nightlife, a charged, blurred and neon world that starts late and finishes as most people wake up. Their shared night world was one of glamorous women as entertainers, waitresses, strippers, hostesses, dancers and even, high-class prostitutes. All very useful providers of information about the targets on Chris's team list.

Only, they're not glamorous when Pup sees them arriving to get ready for work or Tricks sees them at his gym. Most men who slaver over them at midnight would pass them in the street, without a second glance – young Mums and students. Most don't even wear make-up during the day and everything they do wear is loose fitting and sexless. Many are tall and skinny, boyish - skanky even, until they put on the glad rags, the glitter and the glam.

Pup was nearly out of that scene now. Tricks helped Pup, more than anyone but Chris, with his switch from nightclub residencies to corporate functions – and helped him slim down and dry out.

'Have you got the stuff for Skip? I'm seeing Dave and Nick in town tomorrow.'

'Nick's already got it Bud, he was here last night. Flash bastard'

'Flash bastard?' teased Pup, 'You're not exactly easy on the bling yourself.'

'He's the worst kind, he's snake oil – he and Dave have looked down their noses at me for years. Chris never did that but he's always been fucking rich in comparison with us lot. Since Chris fucked off, well … if it wasn't for the girls and you and Scalesy I wouldn't be sorting out the Olympics get together.'

'How did Chris get us all tickets for the main Saturday night of athletics? Those tickets are priceless.' interrupted Pup.

'I asked Trude the same thing. She just said she could hazard a guess but wouldn't and I was never to underestimate Chris's leverage on his contacts – whatever that means'

'It'll be cool Tricks. Are you off the sweeties?'

'Pretty much, as much as you can be in this game'

'Charlie Wright's coming to the Globe – what did you think of her at the tennis?'

'Smart - but a pain in the arse. She's not that much older than my daughter but not as good looking.'

'That's the trouble with you old guys, first the hearing goes then the eyesight ....'

'Cheeky bastard – so ... have you worked out what Chris is doing now? What's he going to do with the stuff I've given him? He'll soon have enough to open his own sweet shop.'

'Well firstly, he's bought it and secondly if he's going to use it himself he's going to make sure he's got enough to do the job. Yeah, I can guess what he's doing - he's building a much bigger collection to leave behind for others for when he's gone'

'Is it safe for him to use Nick as the messenger? After all Nick's been the least active for years and always was up his own arse.'

'Yeah but Skip knows that. He'll be working on the fact that Nick has already taken one lot of presents to him so, even if Nick checks out what's in them, which I suspect he will, then it's a question of who does he trust not to implicate him - Skip or the authorities? After all these years he's going to back Skip to keep him safe, isn't he? Skip will have worked out the odds on all of us.'

'So, what's tomorrow's meet about?'

'Dave wants to make sure that Nick has everything and he wants to ask Scalesy and I some questions so that Nick hears the answers. It's something to do with Skip asking Dave to track down the old landlord of the Spoons pub in Muswell Hill. Remember him?'

'Do I remember him? I nearly lived and died at Spoons in the early days. He was a very, very scary man – someone you never would say 'No' to. I used to sleep on his couch after a Saturday night session and he'd do me a Sunday roast and we'd watch the football on TV, with a few beers and brandy chasers and then we'd do it all again on Sunday night. How he kept it up, how any of us kept it up I dunno.'

'There's one more thing, something that you as a Chelsea fan might be able to do...'

'It depends on the manager as to whether I'm a fan or not and as we have a different manager every other week, I'm not sure if I am a fan this week' said Tricks.

'But the owner stays the same. Roman Abramovich's super yacht, well one of them, he's got five, was in Valletta Grand Harbour in Malta. It's called Titan and is very big. 'Very big' is Skip's technical term for something that's 78 metres long and 3 storeys high with bags

70

of space underneath'. Anyway, Skip has started yacht spotting, like trainspotting, and wants us all to help him. He's started sending me postcards with pictures of locations, hotels and yachts. He wants to know where the world's super yachts are and who will be on them on what dates. Anything we find out, we let Dave know. Dave's in London most weeks now. You know Skip's usual question he wants answering?' asked Pup.

'Who are they fucking?'.

'You got it, Tricks'.

'OK bud, that shouldn't be too difficult – plenty of staff on board or going to entertain. Cocaine isn't just the norm in the square mile it's the week-end choice of all the wealthy. Nick and Scalesy will get as much as me. Now private jets – they're easy'

4.

The letter Chris wrote to Pup in March 2011:

Bonjour Jacques,

Malta is a small island with a small population, think the size of Hull. It is happier, wealthier and more cohesive than most other countries. It will top the European charts on most measures apart from average wages. Everyone seems to know each other through family and friends. It means that jobs, business opportunities, social and political positions can be gained through word of mouth, rather than by formal application. It's like network or referral marketing on a national scale and not a scam like Nick's.

Finding the right medicine to cure your ills is only a matter of asking someone who knows. Even in such long established and powerful social networks the greasing of palms can speed the process. Everyone like a flutter too.

Government officials are accused of accepting bribes, giving favours and receiving back handers from the corporates to succeed in major government contracts, like buildings, transport and energy. Does this matter in a society that continues to move in a good direction? Are the mafia, even the rural mafia in Sicily, any worse than most Governments? It's normal that past or future favours are rewarded. The smoking guns are found by those in the system to eject those that have got too powerful, too greedy and too immoral. The world needs more eco systems like Malta. The US and UK lobbyists are here but on the outside.

Sometimes I read the papers and laugh out loud at how this male dominated country with divisive political allegiances can keep violence and even, occasionally, attempted killings and bombs so under wraps. Perhaps anonymity is guaranteed for the perpetrators if the victims were up to no good.

It is a duopoly but with the Church tending to side with the nationalist party. Back in the day, the church had not allowed Labour Party committee members to take the sacraments. I like their proposed new laws to protect whistle-blowers. There are presidential pardons for the corrupt grassing on other politicians and there was even talk of there being no time limits to those revealed by whistle-blowing.

The protection and momentum behind the 'good' and consistent politicians, many of them part time and having their own businesses, maintains a better balance of power than a government and economy dominated by banks and the big six corporates in each sector. It's not a matter of just getting rid of the bad apples it's about a system that replaces them with good apples

Despite being rated as one of the top countries in the world for quality of life some parts of the establishment are under stress, rather like their trousers. They eat too many pastizzi. The church remains in a state of denial regarding cases of child abuse by priests. This travesty of justice for the victims will remain until large action groups support them and incentives to inform are inside the legal system. I'm rubbish at golf but I can out drive Dave if he has a putter and I have the biggest club in the bag.

Outdoors it is a sunny, friendly community in harmony. It's a make do society. The strength of family and informal networks lessons the reliance on the state. Everyone seems to go to the festivals. Fireworks enthusiasts and band clubs work all year round to make these festivals successful with their displays, including beautiful cribs and models of Bethlehem at Christmas, entertainment and music. Fantastic floats and marching bands aplenty grace the Carnival in Valletta just before Lent. At Easter, there are wonderful processions and displays too. You'd love the models they're so realistic, from buildings to people, from 50 metres away. All the festivals raise money for the church, charities and the band clubs by selling specially prepared, home-made sweetmeats, breads, cakes and chocolate treats. This is crowdfunding par excellence.

Nightly everyone seems to go out walking together, stopping and chatting with friends. Every street, park, beach and square suggests a community enjoying its own company and looking after their own.

Apart from those with the attractive coloured wooden balconies most Maltese homes look small and non-descript from the outside. The masonry may be crumbling and many blocks of newer houses and apartments are so austere they would not look out of place in East Berlin.

Everyone and every dwelling looks crammed together. Massive cranes loom menacingly in every direction you look. There is little respite from the incessant drilling, hacking and shovelling. Wherever you are, on the Maltese coast, you feel in the middle of a never-ending construction site. It's good news for jobs in the building trades and every day new huts and portaloos appear on the horizon to accommodate them.

Yet, inside very many of these unattractive looking dwellings are the most wonderful, spacious and luxuriously decorated and furnished living spaces. Like most countries total domestic harmony is an illusion. Down every street and in every apartment block there is a woman subject to habitual physical or verbal abuse. There's a charity doing some good work to help these victims called Helping Hands. It was founded in 2004.

I think Malta is moving towards a secular society with greater equality. The referendum on divorce was a catalyst and I feel that gay marriage is likely to be allowed if Labour are in power.

Some priests within the Catholic Church threatened 'hell and damnation' to any of their flock that might vote 'Yes' to divorce in the referendum. Posters with a picture of Christ with the words 'Kristu Iva: Divorzju Le (Yes to Christ: No to Divorce) appeared all over Malta. Later the church apologised for the scare tactics, by its priests at the pulpit and in the confessional, but only after all the votes were cast. Despite this and with far more resources spent on advertising and campaigning for the 'No' vote by the governing Nationalist party, the 'Yes', to divorce, vote won. This was much to the surprise of the Government and the Church.

As in Malta half the population go to church regularly this vote does not mean that abortion or cremation will be allowed any day soon. Maltese women will secretly keep going to the UK and Sicily for their abortions and Maltese men will secretly keep visiting the many Thai massage parlours. But this is progress. It is people power through social media. The social media perhaps didn't affect the campaigns but it did give a lot of people confidence that a 'Yes' vote could prevail despite the church, government and conventional media propaganda. No-one ever had to admit going against the Church and the conventions of their society as they could confidentially place their 'Yes' voting slip into the ballot box. It will be the same with the next general election - in 2013.

Citizen Journalism, social media and mass communication through the Internet from the grass roots of society will change opinions and if people are able to vote confidentially then the government, the church, the media and the corporates can all be changed. The US Government can control Google, Apple, Facebook, Amazon and the rest so the citizen journalists need their own channels with their own players. Just like we can play and win on a level playing field in FIFA as an online game but not so much offline at Wembley. Talking of games, the London 2012 game they've developed is hopeless. The graphics are brilliant but the playability is awful. They'll launch it in June but I've got something better ... and free. I'm sure you'll meet Dave's niece, Charlie soon. Charlie is great at promoting new sports players and can help promote my online game too.

There's guys like that New Zealander with his encrypted cloud storage boxes which allows people to collect, store and access media that government authorities can't get to. All is not what it seems. Look at Old Dog Dave and his Missus they are pillars of society. Mrs Dave looks like someone who will let Dave have his rights on the second Friday of the month whereas you and I saw her giving a blow job to our wicketkeeper round the back of the pavilion. Mind, he seemed to catch a lot better that day.

They've even passed laws to say that a cyber-attack on the USA is an act of war and will be retaliated by military intervention. Is that why they always say its China that has hacked the social media, government and payment sites? Everyone knows they won't attack China so perhaps the attacks are from other sources they'd be embarrassed to reveal?

Despite this the citizen journalists and the hackers may be winning the game. In this hyper normalised world, the mainstream has lost their influence and the rich and powerful could be replaced by the unfashionable. It's a gamble, of course, and they'll need a new and powerful engine. Aladdin needs a new lamp rather than a new genie.

Anyway, I'm in the right place. Malta's sunshine, sea, safety, communities, festivals, location, media, technology, i-gaming, pastizzi (as if) and wine – this is the perfect location. If life's a game then this is the best place to play it. In an eclipse, the bigger sun is hidden by the smaller moon and nobody knows what the man in the moon gets up to. I'll send you some postcards of Malta when I can.

Au Revoir Jacques

Ernest Defarge

Three old newspaper clippings from the Malta Times were enclosed with this letter to Pup:

The first newspaper report told the tragic story of a fireworks factory explosion in Gozo. The explosion had wiped out an entire family; father, two sons, daughter in law, son in law and a family friend. The distraught mother watched from an upstairs window as the coffins, each with an identifying photograph, were carried in procession to the church.

It had been impossible to be sure if the right remains were in each coffin. The mother was quoted as being angry that the feast that the 'enthusiasts' were preparing the fireworks for went ahead. She felt it should have been cancelled as a mark of respect.

The article stated that twenty-four people, in Gozo alone, had died in fireworks–related disasters. The prevalent view was that no government would dare stop the production of fireworks by the enthusiasts. The fireworks and the enthusiasts, the hobbyists that produce them, are a major part of Maltese life. Each town and village will have many feast days each year. Sliema has five with the fireworks being set off from large rafts and boats in the sea. There are many other major national celebrations, all of which are 'embellished' by fireworks.

The second cutting was also about fireworks. It implied that, because of a tip off to the police; a man may have been framed for illegal storage of fireworks. The heading was 'A miscarriage of justice' These were the words of a 41-year-old trumpeter that had been convicted, with a two-year prison sentence, for storing explosives in the basement of the Naxxar Peace Band Club.

The convicted man said he had no interest in fireworks although he was passionate about the feasts' decorations. He held the key to the basement store but claimed he had no knowledge of a small room that was found to be packed with explosives. The entrance to this room was totally hidden by a tall white cupboard.

He stored paint in the cupboard but showed photographs which seemed to prove that no-one standing in the basement store could see another entrance. Indeed, two previous police searches, before the successful one, had not revealed the secret room and the man was adamant that he did not know of its existence.

The third report suggested another frame up. It involved explosives but on a much more terrible scale. It was a well-known story about the Lockerbie bombing.

It stated that 100 Maltese nationals, along with nationals from 32 other countries, had signed a petition calling on the Scottish government to open an independent inquiry into the only Lockerbie (December 1988) bombing conviction to date. The petitioners' spokesperson was Jim Swire, the father of Flora, a victim of the worst terrorist act on British soil.

It is claimed that Mr Al-Megrahi, who at the time was a Libyan secret service agent working with Libyan Arab airlines in Malta, had nothing to do with the bomb – 'a gross miscarriage of justice'. Investigators concluded that the bomb that exploded over Scotland was loaded in unaccompanied luggage on an Air Malta flight to Germany before making its way to London. The luggage was traced back to Mr Al-Megrahi. The 'highly suspect' yet crucial evidence to convict him was provided by a Maltese shopkeeper who identified him as the person who bought the clothes that were found in the luggage. Mr Al-Megrahi's defence, and the reason for the petition, is that the Maltese shopkeeper was paid 'more than $2 million' while his brother was paid more than '$1 million' for 'cooperating'. Neither man has ever denied receiving these massive sums.

CHAPTER FIVE: It's Bin Laden's Fault

Opaque: Hard to understand: obscure and unintelligible in meaning

1.

AFTER LEAVING PEAK HEALTH GYM, Pup had taken the tube to Kensington High Street. He was performing that lunchtime, for a room full of accountants, at an Awards Ceremony at Kensington Roof Gardens. The Roof Gardens are owned by Sir Richard Branson's Virgin Group and hired out to corporates for private functions. Pup had done gigs there before and was looking forward to it. It paid well; he'd be away by 3.30 and at the Magic Circle, near Euston, by 4pm. He knew his act was perfect for this audience.

His equipment had gone on before him with Will who was his mate, driver, techie and stooge. Will would set up everything before the delegates arrived. Stormy may look like any other pool playing, wooden doll in a tuxedo, until the mouth, eyes, arms and cue move with Pup 20 metres away working the tables – animatronics – Chris's idea.

2.

Chris had walked through the park, rather than stay on the promenade. He'd made the diversion to get his daily fix of amusement. He was now in Independence Park, Sliema. The tree and hedge lined park is long and narrow and is sandwiched between, on one side, the rocks and sea and, on the other, the promenade and main road.

This part of Sliema is one of the most sought after residential areas in Malta. It is where many of the best hotels and most expensive apartments are. The beautiful people with their designer clothes and footwear can be seen power walking, jogging, parading and promenading from early morning to late at night. Chris did none of this but enjoyed watching them. The different speeds, sounds, gestures, wobbles, sizes, gaits, snorts, expressions, wet patches, smells and self-consciousness amused him more than any play or film. The promenade meanders for about three miles from Tigne Point, through Sliema, Baluta, St Julian's Bay and finishes at Spinola Bay.

At one end of the long, narrow, tree lined, park is Dixie's open-air café. Dixie's is one of Chris's favourite cafes and not just because Mr. Dixie had placed the apostrophe in the correct place on his sign. At the other end of the park is a children's playground.

The humans share the park with fifty or more stray cats. They are extremely well fed and well looked after stray cats. The cats have their own posh hotels, shelters with bedding and plentiful food and drink, all donated by the Sliema residents. These Sliema cats and humans are more cosmopolitan than elsewhere in Malta - all colours, ages, races and beliefs.

It's not clear whose park it is – the cats or the humans. On balance, Chris thought it was the cats' park as nearly every bench seat and table had a cat. It was mandatory for humans, certainly for those that want peace and quiet, to stroke, tickle, rub, play with and feed their nearest cat.

Chris was an avid people watcher. Many elderly couples spent most of their days together in this park. Each couple would have their own routine for the day. Chris was curious, envious even, as to why couples would want to spend their last years in this way. Why would so many want to be in such proximity? Was that how they'd spent the whole of their life – holidaying, breakfasting, lunching, dinnering, cycling, swimming, walking, watching and sleeping together? Did they love each other's company so much? Was being together all the time by choice or by circumstance? Did they know why?

There was one retired English couple, clearly living in Malta, which Chris never tired of watching. He admired them greatly as he'd never had such a calm, settled, content, relationship as he assumed their relationship was.

Nothing in Chris's life was calm now. He raged about everything and couldn't stop his mind thinking of something else to rage about. Just spotting a political poster, catching a headline in a newspaper or a thought about one of his targets would bring about another rage. He'd be walking along the street and inside his head he'd shout 'Fuck'. In public loos he found himself mouthing the words he'd say to one of his targets if he met them. It was embarrassing.

He couldn't even rely on himself to do the ordinary things simply and properly. Panic was never far away. He'd find his kettle in the fridge. One day he walked out the apartment and across a pedestrian crossing before he realised he was wearing his PJ bottoms. To be sure not to lose his apartment keys he always has five sets in stock and each day places three sets in different places - bag, hat and back pocket -so that he'll always be able to get back in should he lose some.

Routine just wasn't possible anymore for Chris. Although he'd always been a loner he now felt desperately alone. So, there were so many things to admire in the way this couple got through the day. Their companionship and peace with life were both unattainable for Chris but he never tired of watching them.

The timing and sequence of their daily activities were perfectly replicated. Chris varied the time he entered the park and guessed correctly where each would be in the sequence. The woman always looked content, serene, impeccably dressed, slim, tanned but never too much flesh exposed, short grey hair, designer glasses, straight backed and focused. She seemed to happily and untiringly ingest novel after novel. Chris had never seen her lose her concentration, her focus on the words.

This focus was a remarkable achievement. Serene Lady was never distracted by jumping, skating, stone throwing, biking, tumbling, sobbing, wailing and screaming kids. She never looked up to watch the cooing, coaxing, cajoling and admonishing grandparents. She never shut her book in exasperation from the noise of the pram-wheeling, buggy-pushing, swing pushing, chattering and shouting parents. She never seemed to lose her train of thought as around her feet assembled lizards, fallen kids, over excited dogs and the park's elite guard, of at least one hundred, cats in a variety of superior poses.

Twice in the day this couple would visit the café. They made one or two drinks last for hours. He would do the crossword or suck his pen and listen to his iPod. Serene Lady would recommence reading her novel.

From early to late afternoon they'd move a good fifty metres further up the park. If the cats allowed them, they'd settle at their favourite, adjacent benches. He did not look serene, like his wife, but looked very friendly yet lumpy. Lumpy Lad dressed more like a tourist with the almost obligatory baseball hat to complete the look and for protection too. As his wife resumed her reading position on one bench he would lie down, often flat on his back, sometimes on his side, knees bent, on the other. Within seconds Lumpy Lad was asleep and would stay asleep for forty minutes.

How Chris envied the fact that this man never snored and looked so content in his afternoon nap. Chris could never nap and every night he snored, sweated, hallucinated and woke himself up with the shouting inside his head. Lately he'd seen his mother standing at the end of his bed. She was wearing the nightie she'd worn on the night she died in hospital. Her oxygen mask was dangling from one ear. He heard her complaint, it was always the same, and he always responded to it angrily. By the time his alarm went off at seven each morning he was totally exhausted.

Meanwhile, Serene Lady, on the adjacent bench to the silently sleeping Lumpy Lad, would continue reading her novel. Late in the afternoon the couple would return to the café. He would resume his crossword and she, her novel. They only spoke when they moved locations. At 5.30 each day they left the park, together of course, stopping off at the grocery shop near their apartment.

One-day Lumpy Lad nodded at Chris and Serene Lady said 'Hello'. Chris was shocked that they recognised him. They'd probably been watching him and were curious about why he was watching them.

One day, Chris counted twelve elderlies, expat couples in the park. They were reading, sleeping or staring into space. Many couples had synchronised movements. They'd take off their sunglasses or a layer of clothing at the same time. They'd take a sip of water at the same time. Chris's favourite was when each raised an ice-cream cone to their mouth at the same time.

When they shuffled away together from their benches, many would hold hands. Each couple would rarely speak but they'd always remain side by side. Chris mused that all the best blues songs used train images – 'People get ready there's a train a coming. You don't need no ticket – you just get on board'. Maybe these elderly couples were just waiting together at the station for that final train journey? Chris couldn't wait around; he had too much to do.

Chris stopped at the park administration and public toilets block. This was where the park's free Wi-Fi zone was. Young people of all nationalities were on the benches outside the block, shading their laptops, netbooks, tablets and smartphones from the sun.

Maltese music was blaring out of the toilets and a well-dressed, middle-aged man was sat outside. He was on hand to keep everything clean and to provide toilet paper for those that required it. But mainly he was just whiling away the hours chatting to friends that dropped by, whilst collecting his tips in a small bowl.

Chris thought to himself that was the kind of job he'd have liked. His lack of a sense of smell would have been useful but he would have raged at all the men that left without washing their hands. As Chris had spent a lifetime counting things and working out proportions and percentages he realised he'd be raging at over 80% of the men. This, Chris concluded, might not be a good idea in the caretaking of public conveniences business.

Chris didn't use the toilet but went straight to the mirror. He hardly recognised himself clean-shaven. He checked that his scars were fully covered. He considered his eyes in the mirror and surprised himself to see tears forming. Within seconds, the tears rolled down his cheeks until he could taste the saltiness on his lips. 'That's a new one', he thought, 'Hell, I must be fucking lonely'.

Chris went back outside and took his iPad out of his red bag to do some work on his 'Open Shutter' blog. After a few minutes, he shut it down and put it back in the bag. Out of the bag he took his fountain pen and the leather-bound book with the magnetic clasp. He wrote:

Don't you just love this neat little brown and gold book? I think it's a bit special. It says it is bound in 'hand tooled leather capturing the flavour of finely wrought Renaissance style bindings'. It has a clever little black wrap round magnetic strap to keep everything together. Well Steph, at least it's a bit more personal than a memory stick. If you've read up to this point you're about half way through. I'm sure you're annoyed by the poor grammar and punctuation but I'm in a bit of a rush now and there isn't time to revise – so not my usual standard.

Here's a clipping of a press photograph I've kept for a long while now. It was a big shock when I first saw it. Can you see the woman, with her face in her hand, the hair, her eyes – can you see why, just for an instant, I thought it was you? She's Nigerian and only 25 (did you spot the compliment?). Tragically she'd just laid her sister to rest. She'd escaped Libya by boat. On the way to Lampedusa, that's the Italian island that along with Malta has been the favourite destination for tens of thousands of boat people, the engine broke down. The boat started to drift. She said that many planes and boats had seen them but only a Malta vessel, after 3 days, stopped and brought them ashore.

There were many reports of big boats pushing these tiny boats back towards Libya. The number of deaths at sea ran into thousands. Horribly, and I can imagine how desperate it was, some of them, including her pregnant sister, drank seawater. Her sister died as a result.

It was only one of many tragedies and they're still going on post Gaddafi. But tell me Steph how could we have condoned all the US and UK air force and naval presence, there on humanitarian grounds, not helping the thousands of people dying at sea trying to flee Libya? Why is our bombing of innocent citizens, anywhere in the world, including with unmanned drones, not a war crime?

They've learned that the humanitarian pretext is a lot easier to use than the bombing countries in self-defence – weapons of mass destruction et al. Of course, the rebels cause as many crimes on humanity as the regime but no-one ever counts the civilians killed and tortured by the 'good guys', Syria is far worse, and a better case for humanitarian intervention, but they let that go on and on.

Anyway, it's all Bin Laden's fault. Getting rid of him gave them license to do anything they wanted. LOL about the first story of a forty-five-minute firefight in the 'fog' of action accompanied by a picture of Obama, Hillary Clinton et al watching the raid live on a monitor in the White House. Presumably by 'fog' they meant the stun grenades they used on Bin Laden's invisible security guards. There must have been a real pea souper in the room where they were watching it. Neat original bit of PR to release a photo of them watching it live. No one cared that what they claimed they'd seen live they admitted later didn't happen.

Oh well, that's life in the movies, so, later we find out he was unarmed, not hiding behind anyone and the wounded woman, not his wife, was caught in crossfire between the Seals.

Every new book and film that comes out using Seals testimonies and documents, supposedly found in Bin Laden's place, is an insult to our intelligence – but they don't care.

We need our own media, not controlled by Corporate America, that we can present our own daily films. I think Moore was right in 'Bowling for Columbine'. It is the images in the media, which so frighten the population about their own wellbeing, that makes America so aggressive. They'll always lead the rankings on gun crime, blowing countries up and stamping out anyone or anything that is different.

All this scaremongering, by the establishment, from baddies in foreign lands to foods that might kill you, is done to make Corporate America richer. The American Dream is a nightmare and the pursuit of it leads to despair and debt. Debt is the way they control all of us. For the few – riches. For the many - indebtedness and fear. There are few winners and many losers. The shocker for me was to see that Lockheed don't just supply the weapons of mass destruction they also run the US Welfare to Work programme. This, like ours, is a programme to segregate and humiliate the poor to the point of ill health, addiction and crime – where corporate America can benefit some more. Where America leads we follow. Big corporate money can get any poser elected as President of the US and then they stay in power by appointing their four thousand strong administration. It's different in Britain but the day will come when a puppet Prime Minister can act like a dictator too. I can't imagine the stress you're under Steph, being a part of all these inhumane policies, day after day.

To the big, swinging dicks funding Saddam, Gaddafi, Bin Laden, and then changing the deal on them, it is just fabulously good business. It's a high cost in lives – just think of how many more are dying and oppressed in Libya and Iraq now that Gadaffi and Saddam aren't there but lives aren't a cost to US business. Each time you change a regime you're a winner - you get the oil, the energy deals, the loans deals, the arms deals, the pharmaceutical deals, the fast food deals and the reconstruction deals too.

It's fucking pathetic, Steph. For the last, nigh on 30 years I've been paying people to expose the hypocrites, even to the point of resignation, but still they come. It's too bloody late exposing the propaganda and the hypocrites after the damage is done. Wikileaks is no bloody good either – it's all after the event – I tell you no ruddy…

The raging and the effort involved in writing this down were draining Chris of his energy. He wanted to tell Steph more about his project so that she would respect him but he knew that, for today, he had nothing left. He'd over used his inhaler. He could hardly keep his eyes open and even when he tried to focus, what he'd written was blurred. He'd start again in the morning. He hated not telling everything to Steph but there was no option. He knew what he was doing was for the right reasons and all he could do was give her those reasons and hope that she understood when she found out what he'd done.

He decided to walk further on through Independence Park to watch the sun set. With luck his adopted cat, Mr. Bojangles, would be there too. He'd called the cat Mr. Bojangles not because this cat could dance or 'jump so high' but because of the line in the song about Bojangles' dog of fifteen years. The line was that the dog 'just upped and died'. Mr. Bojangles had this same effect on dogs.

This was a large white cat with brown markings; one was on his tail and another as a patch, over one eye. When an unsuspecting, excitable dog spied Mr. Bojangles in his favourite sleeping spot, in the hedgerow, naturally it would bark and prepare for the chase. Mr. Bojangles did not like his sleep being disturbed.

It was a great shock to the dog, of any size, to see this large white cat advancing in slow, measured strides towards it. Mr. Bojangles also had a whole range of hard cat gimmicks as he approached the ring.

Two of these gimmicks turned every dog's blood to ice. Mr. Bojangles would paw the air with each claw in turn whilst making the most fearful loud hissing sound. The dog immediately understood that Mr. Bojangles was not amused and, worse, was a seeker of a dog damaging, vengeance.

The dog would stop barking and for a second would freeze, with tongue flopped out uselessly and eyes staring incredulously.

Then, sensibly, the dog would turn to leave. The dog's pace would then quicken considerably as he realised that he was being followed, at Usain Bolt-like speed, by Mr. Bojangles. Less than ten seconds later the humans and cats in the park would hear the familiar, anguished sounds of mauled dog. The dog probably survives. Mr. Bojangles is unscathed. He struts back, in measured strides, to resume his place and sleep in the shade of the hedgerow.

Sat on their bench overlooking St Julian's Bay, Mr. Bojangles and Chris watch a ten-metre-wide, strip of sunlight. It is at least a mile long. It starts from the highest point on the horizon - the top of the blue Portamoso tower. It travels down through the dusk and then rides on the waves of the dark sea to rest directly below them. They are the chosen ones.

3.

Pup was thinking about sex again. He was thinking about meeting Charlie soon. He knew they were in love even though they'd never really spoken to each other. He knew he should be preparing to go on stage, visioning his act and illusions. But here he was walking around the gardens, looking across the rooftops and down below to the frenzy and frustration of people worried about how they look and whether they'd be late.

He loved this place, the French Garden, the Spanish Garden, the English Garden, saying hello to the flamingos and cocktails in the Silver Bar. He wondered what the rest of the Richardsons would say when he went home tonight with plans to turn the flat roof extension at 94 Sunningfields Road into a garden attraction.

Thinking about sex recalled Chris's belief that pleasure was always more powerful than threat or torture. Most of what Chris had found out about the people in power he'd learned from those that give them pleasure. Once when Pup was at his lowest, Chris told him he was thinking too much. Working life and monogamy are about repression but sex is about escapism. Lust was too powerful for even the most powerful to control.

Pup, had seen for years when he'd been the resident MC at the Stork Club, just how champagne, cocaine and sex fuels the City of London. Male discretion vanishes in the instant of the hostess or dancer loosening their belt or unzipping their fly. Presumably, Pup thought, his father, Geoff, will have enjoyed these extra-curricular activities with his clients but although Geoff and Pup were well off – they were never in the league of Chris and Nick. A Gold Amex card was the key to unlock any door in London in 1984 and Chris and Nick's stories on tour that year were legendary.

Chris made out that his job as a European HR Director, mainly involved negotiating deals to hire talent they needed, whilst settling with those executives they summarily dismissed and smoothing over all the indiscretions of the top executives – particularly in-company indiscretions where the woman would be compensated for leaving. Chris always said the reason there was a glass ceiling was because the men above it didn't want women seeing how they spend their time.

Chris believed that the reason for his continued high earnings, continually being headhunted and longevity - right through to early retirement at fifty-five - was that he couldn't be fired. Chris always knew too much. The reason he knew too much was that he always asked the women, he was asked to placate or move on, what they'd found out about the executive.

To prove his theory that pleasure is a faster way to the truth than pain. Chris had told Pup of the Dom, to the rich and powerful, that he knew when he was in 'Corporatedumb', as he used to term it. He started by saying 'Think of the top tennis stars, the top formula one stars, the top footballers, top footballers, top actors and top pop stars. Think how much they must get on an hourly performance basis - now double it. One hour for her to humiliate you.'

On entering her suite an attractive slave would entertain the client. Entertainment could take the form of massage, drink, food, drugs, videos, music, dance, fellatio, jacuzzi and sauna - whatever helped the client to relax. When relaxed she'd bathe him and then put a black leather hood over him. The apertures for the eye and nose were quite large but the opening for the mouth had a gold zip. Dependent on the forthcoming entertainment, the slave would either put leather handcuffs on him, to secure his wrists behind his back, or a leather restraint that secured his wrists to the very top of his thighs. She would then lead him into her Mistress's room.

There were a few instruments of play, or pain, on display but this was not a dungeon. It was a very warm and sumptuously furnished boudoir. Standing in front of the client was a slim, tall, and naked, apart from diamond necklace, drop earrings, black silk gloves, stockings and heels, young woman. There was a professional cameraman there too. Such was the fame of this Dom amongst the rich and powerful that a film to show your rich and powerful friends, or jerk off to, was an additional feature of the entertainment package. The cameraman always stayed out of the client's eye line.

She looked so damn good, slim, and almost skinny, long legs, pert, small breasts, and clit ring, black, short hair in a fringe, dark blue eye shadow, long black eyelashes and red, gloss lipstick. She spoke in an affected, smoky, mellow, and warm but always sounding slightly curious voice. She was English but each word was enunciated as if she had only just learned but liked the sound of it. The last syllable always went higher – as if a question. It usually wasn't - it was an instruction. Each instruction was short – one to three words.

She was, in heels, taller than most of her clients. She maintained eye contact from his first coming into the room. The guy would come before she'd said a word, usually within seconds of his entering the room. After being secured against a wall she walked slowly to him. A slap of his cock, a squeeze of his balls and a slow pull down between finger and thumb as if testing whether the cock could disappear into the balls – and that was it. The Dom would walk away slowly a few metres and stop with her back to him whilst the slave girl would clean him up and then leave. The Dom then turned around and said to her client 'Now… I play'.

She seemed to do everything in slow motion. For minutes, nothing would happen at all. Then when with her client standing, maintaining eye contact throughout, she'd hold his cock until it was hard – then look at it and then slap it hard. Painful I should imagine. Whenever she got his cock hard, she'd often do nothing for minutes, even walk away to smoke a cigarette. Then she'd return and squeeze his balls – hard, slap his cock – hard and whip his cock and balls – hard. She'd insert a silver needle into his urethra – very slowly. She'd turn and put his cock between her thighs, brushing her vagina but holding the end so he couldn't move.

She'd sit on the couch with him on his knees in front of her, she'd open her legs and bring his cock to her vagina and she'd order him to 'Push' but his cock was never allowed beyond her lips. In fact, he never would get to penetrate her.

Her finishing moves usually involved him on his back, again unable to move, and her straddling his face with her back to him so that her gloved hands could play with his cock. She may put his cock to her cheek and just hold it there. Every now and then she'd open the gold zip on his hood and say 'Lick'. Once, maybe twice she'd open the gold zip, hold his mouth open and piss in it. Near the end of the allotted time, still straddling the client the Dom would stroke his cock to the climax of pressing his cock to her breast and he'd explode. She would then walk out the room and he'd never see her again.

Chris made the point that the client was always so desperate to come or for a blowjob, or to penetrate her that had she rewarded him with that in exchange for the answer to any question – she could get any question answered. She was more powerful than Prime Minister, Margaret Thatcher. They nicknamed her Top Cat because she topped all the Fat Cats.

Pup always wondered whether life would bring him his own Top Cat but he knew such fantasies must be bought – they don't exist in real life. Then again, Charlie was tall, slim, dark haired and fit – Pup could but hope.

4.

Steph didn't like it when the Chamberpots ignored her, when it all went quiet. She knew that, to them, she was ultimately Chris's lover and a representative of Her Majesty's Government but she'd hoped that over nearly fifteen years she would have built their trust. Trude, especially Trude, lived within half an hour's walk from Steph and they got on well.

Had she offended her on the train trip back from the tennis? Did she ask Trude too many questions about what Chris might be doing? Did Trude know from Chris that Steph had cooled their relationship? Did she think that if they were no longer an item, there was no reason for Steph to continue to attend Chamberpots get-togethers? To Steph that would be just horrible – she was so looking forward to the Globe and then the Olympics. These were her friends.

Steph had contacted Scalesy and agreed to meet him for coffee. Scalesy was always helpful, always straight – a kind, intelligent and honest man with a lovely sense of humour. He'd understand if Steph needed re-assuring about how it was all going to end.

Steph was in London in the Victoria and Westminster area. Although Scalesy's most famous clients were in Buckinghamshire, the majority were in Central London, so it was easy to fix a date. Scalesy suggested a day when he was going to meet with Dave and Nick so that if there was anything Steph needed sorting with the others he could do it straight away.

Scalesy, suggested they had breakfast at an old school Italian café close to Westminster tube station and across the road from the Houses of Parliament. Scalesy was reading Metro at a table but had waited for Steph to arrive before ordering. They both had espressos. Scalesy had a croissant. Steph had yoghurt and fruit. Before Scalesy had taken the first bite of his croissant, Steph handed him her iPad saying: 'Have you seen this?' It was one of Chris's 'Open Shutter' blogs. Steph said: Do you know how to scroll it down… oh I'm sorry Scalesy, of course you do'.

'No worries' said Scalesy and quickly read the blog.

CORPORATE FRAUD WILL DROWN US ALL

It is a mistake to think the world is imploding from natural disasters and US, UK and France supported military interventions. For the cause of the implosion one need look no further than the beneficiaries of these environmental and human disasters. Major US corporations and their UK supporters are the cause.

No matter who lights the blue touch paper it is these major corporations that are the preferred suppliers of the fire extinguisher. Sudan, Syria, Bahrain, Yemen, Mali, Nigeria, Ivory Coast, Iraq, Mauritania, Tunisia, Egypt, Afghanistan, Libya and Tunisia are easy to light the blue touch paper and so, to these Corporations, are immediate market opportunities. Every now and again they must change the management team in these countries to maximise the earnings potential.

It took me many years to understand that the media fill their pages and air space with the words and actions of politicians, which allows the puppet masters to remain hidden from view. Career politicians become very wealthy people because of being the communicators of the Corporates. That is just the way it works. It is why, whichever politicians form a government the result is always the same, for, inexorably, their purpose in governing is to protect the assets of those that sponsored them and ensure the rich get richer and the poor get poorer. No US or UK Government has bucked this trend for 30 years.

The only way for Western society to evolve more positively is to find a process to elect new rule makers. Current democracies only perpetuate the status quo. The world is ruled by these corporates and so our world is drowning in corporate fraud.

Over the last decade every Wall Street firm has paid big fines for all sorts of crimes including outright embezzlement by their CEOs. A few years since the biggest financial crisis in history not a single financial leader in the UK or US has faced jail. The bigger you are and the more trouble you get into the greater the certainty you'll be bailed out.

Most of the corrupt bosses are still in position and getting fatter on their mammoth salaries, perks and bonuses. They run the IMF that is as dodgy as all the financial institutions they run. What is worse, because it's a matter of life and death, they are the ones that make the decisions about which regime, that has got the oil or natural resource they want, is to be supported. Not surprising that the first sale of oil by the Rebel Council was to Qatar and yet it all went to the US to be processed.

The US hated that Gaddafi had National Oil to sort out profit sharing terms with global oil companies, worse he was talking to China and India, and worse still was threatening to get rid of the current system and distribute oil revenue directly to the people. It was an imperative for Corporate America that they privatised the Libyan Oil industry.

It's not just oil though. Blowing up a country, getting control of it and putting it back together again is just fantastic business. Tomahawk missiles cost $1.5 million dollars each. At least 4000 missions are needed to blow somewhere like Libya up but it still represents a good investment. US Arms sales are increasing at 50% per annum, technology, construction, medical, loans and financial services- all are going up and up.

They make so many $Billions they can afford to admit to the Senate that over $60billion in cash went missing that they'd lent for Iraq's reconstruction. The corporates don't get rich by conventional trading they get rich by being very good at acquisition, speculation, gambling, fraud and corruption. Voters do not understand the numbers.

For example, organised crime in Italy, primarily cocaine, is reckoned to be worth £160 billion a year. It sounds a lot until I realised that it is about the same turnover as Italy's largest energy company and less than one per cent of the amount accumulated by legitimate US and UK financial services companies from their proven mis-selling of financial services products and investments.

In other words, corporate fraud pays over a hundred times better than organised crime. Both the leaders of the organised crime and the legitimate financial services industry believe, despite the destruction, deaths and poverty they cause, that it is 'only business' and there is little chance of them being punished.

Don't think it's done for all the shareholders either, it's mainly done for the Chairmen, the CEOs, the executive directors, a few non-executive directors and a few controlling, institutional, shareholders. They avoid taxation because they pay other corporates in the club to do that for them. All the top 100 corporates switch accountants from time to time but it is still the same five accountancy giants that share all their business. No need for conspiracy theories about tax laws or tax avoidance.

Corruption pays big time. Look at Rick Scott, Governor of Florida or Steve Rattner. When Obama wanted someone to help with the bail out of the Automobile industry he chose Rattner to fix ii even though Rattner was under investigation for

93

giving kickbacks to government officials. Of course, he settled his own case for a few million dollars.

That's the point though, isn't it? If they get caught they settle but they've still done nicely out of the corruption. Vice President Cheney set the precedent, before he became Vice President of the USA and Head of Acquisition of Iraq's oilfields. He proved that they'd never take on the biggest multinationals. While he was CEO of Halliburton, his firm engaged in illegal bribery of Nigerian officials to enable them to win access to that country's oil fields. Getting access was worth billions of dollars and certainly worth a paltry out of court settlement of $35 million.

Half the US Congress are millionaires and very many have ties to the Corporates before they arrive in Congress. The UK has gone the same way, although many make the multi millions after they leave office.

I thought that 'Bowling for Columbine', Michael Moore's film, concluded that what made America many more times violent with its guns, than any other country, was the images of fear that its media propagates. This fear, putting a whole country under stress, is in the interest of and therefore promoted by the Corporates.

Whilst maximising income in the US by promoting fear of crime, obesity, cancer and so forth the same Corporates are turning in record sales and profits by promoting different messages, even the opposite messages, in other countries. Cigarette sales are increasing worldwide yet millions die from smoking. Prescription drugs, oil spills, radiation and technology cause more deaths but the corporates maximise the revenue earning opportunity in the countries that allow them to get away with it.

It is probably two generations after the event that society finds out about the millions that have died because of the Corporates lobbying and getting legislation that enables their mass marketing of products that may be detrimental to health – from technology to foods. The only sure thing is that when they do find out the perpetrators are incredibly wealthy and their lawyers settle – no one gets locked up.

The West's leading politicians are regularly invited to hold secret talks with the wealthiest Chairmen, Owners and CEOs of America's largest Global Corporates. This is the ruling class not the group that has been elected to govern.

The ruling class will congregate at the Koch Brothers annual two days get together of America's wealthiest individuals, or within the Carlyle Group, Bilderberg, Buffet and Gates' Billionaires Club, FIFA, the International Olympics Committee and so forth.

There are lifebelts to prevent our drowning. The way to change all this, getting the ruling class to act differently is through citizen journalism and whistle-blowers. But it must be about what they plan to do, not just what they've done. We must have politicians with a long consistent record of positive values and integrity ready to replace the corrupt. The through social media and word of mouth we need the momentum of a movement to get them elected to replace the corrupt. When voters understand the scale of the crime and the suffering, for the few to prosper, they will mandate new governments led by politicians with integrity to prosecute all individuals for corporate fraud. When the judiciary has no alternative but to send individuals to jail for corporate crimes then the ruling class may modify their behaviour.

YOURS FAITHFULLY,
OPEN SHUTTER

Scalesy put his reading glasses back in a leather case and looked quizzically at Steph and asked:

'So, what's different between this and the Skip's other blogs?'

'I think you know Scalesy. The last two paragraphs are a call to arms. He's not just looking to expose those he considers hypocrites. He's looking to expose the most powerful men, and a few women, in the world. He as good as names them. He's never done that before. Is this what all this frenetic Chamberpots activity is about? Is he trying to get to these people? Many of them will be at the London Olympics – what is he going to do to them. This is out of your league, Scalesy.'

'Whoa. Steady Steph. You know him better than any of us. Why do you think, nearly 30 years ago, he formed the Lord Chamberlain's men?'

'Because he wanted to level the playing field and a few baddies to resign would do that?'

'Partly, but the main reason was that we were all angry. We were all furious that the pictures on our television screens about the miners' strike were purely government propaganda. It's strange that in April 2012, when you and I carry at least two devices on us that can take instant pictures and movies of everything that happens, we're still angry about the propaganda in the media.'

95

'So, you're saying it's not just about Chris?'

'What Chris has done, or at least what he's tried to do, is to keep us honest. He is obsessive and can be very boring but he only deals in fact. His blogs are just a way of reminding us, all the journalists and film makers he's sponsored, and the influencers of the politicians, that exposing the truth is a damned good idea. He's also saying that it's not enough. Those that are to be exposed must be replaced by people with integrity and value that make them appropriate for power.'

'But what are you up to, Scalesy? If you don't level with me I'll have to let my bosses know – so that they can find out.'

'That's cool Steph but remember we never do anything illegal and we've only ever supplied information to Chris. How old is Chris? Late sixties, I guess, I doubt if he's going to start being a baddie now either.'

'That's not very helpful, Scalesy'

'Put it another way then. Since 1984 the only people that know what information we've passed to Chris are me, Dave, Trude, Pup, Tricks and Nick. We don't even know what the others have passed on to Chris. When you read about the scandals of MP expenses, secret government deals with media and lobbyists, government contractors making millions for naff all, you don't know if it's Chris behind it or Private Eye or that investigative journalists' association or just a great idea they had themselves – and neither do we.'

'So ...?'

'So, I'm saying, do you trust the man you love, to not do anything to harm us? I do and that's why I'll continue to help him until he dies. I'm sure he won't raise a finger to the establishment at the Olympics or anywhere.'

'OK Scalesy, but aren't you worried that something has changed him. Nick called him a 'loose cannon'.'

'Not everyone helps Chris just because they trust him. For many years, some Chamberpots have been scared stiff of what Chris could and couldn't do to them. Sometimes we are a coalition of the unwilling. The fact that Chris is dying and is choosing what he wants to do before he dies, scares them even more, but it shouldn't scare you'.

'You don't seem worried that I might have to tell my bosses?'

'Chris thinks someone has told your bosses years ago. From time to time he's sure he's being followed. It could be paranoia but I doubt it. Since 1984 he's been prepared to be questioned by the establishment and all his data seized. He wouldn't be surprised if everything he's said, typed or written has been monitored. Personally, I think he'll be disappointed if he isn't ever questioned. Knowing our Skip, he'll hand them a script for his interrogation. He's always had his lawyer friends on standby. I don't think you have anything to worry about. If you are worried tell your bosses – Chris would understand'.

'So, are you a reluctant Chamberpot, Scalesy?'

'No, Steph, I'm not. Getting to know Chris and all our Chamberpots get-togethers has been terrific fun. I wouldn't be as successful without the encouragement Chris has given me and the clients that he's put my way. I've never been asked by Chris to do anything that I don't feel comfortable with doing. I've done nothing illegal or wrong. I'm going to really, really miss him when he goes. Aren't you?'

'Of course.'

'Then lighten up Steph – we've got The Globe then the Olympics to look forward to. You shall go to the ball and I'll be delighted to accompany you.'

CHAPTER SIX: The Aristocrats

Embed: to become deeply lodged or assign reporter to military
unit

1.

PUP KNEW IT WAS CRAZY to be walking around the Roof gardens in his tuxedo and Peyton shoes but his shirt was wet with perspiration. He hoped that a walk in the sunshine, with his jacket slung over his shoulder, would dry it. There was at least half an hour to go. It was stiflingly hot in the Club Room where he'd be performing and he would only go in there when he heard his name announced and his entrance music.

For now, he was talking to the four resident flamingos in the English garden. He liked the Moorish flavour of the Spanish garden best but he preferred the flamingos to the lavender, lilacs, roses, evergreens, crocuses, anemones and all the other listed flowers and shrubs.

Pup hadn't a clue, which was which. He wondered whether old people, that could identify all this foliage, developed an interest in gardening when other pursuits became just too bothersome or whether, at a certain age, they just remembered what they'd been told about flowers and shrubs by their parents.

'Hello Bill, Hello Ben, Hello Splosh and Hello Pecks' said Pup, saluting each flamingo in turn.

'Hi Stevo. You could have joined us if you'd had your flip flops on', said Pecks, the only one of the four showing any interest in Pup.

'Sorry Pecks, I have a show to do.'

'Not with that foul mouthed Stormy I hope?'

'Fraid so Pecks – he gets more laughs than me.'

'Aw – we'll laugh at you Stevo.'

'Are you alright, Sir?'

Pup turned around to see the questioner. A young man in overalls, kneeling with trowel in hand, looking up, concerned.

'Ah…. Yes, thanks …. Just having a chat with my manager' said Pup and hurriedly walked on.

2.

Charlie was thinking about her meeting with her Uncle, Sir Nigel in York. The more she thought about it the less angry she became. She hadn't been in the right mood to see him anyway what with Dave denying that he'd been in the Royal York Hotel. She was certain it was him. She had no idea why her personal affairs should be of any interest to her Uncle Nigel or Uncle Dave or why her father was mentioned. It was clear that Sir Nigel would make it worth her while to move back to London, effect a conciliation with her husband and then quietly arrange a divorce.

On reflection Charlie didn't mind being bought off as she'd felt that her marriage had been arranged in the first place. It was not quite a Princess Di and Camilla situation but not far off. What Charlie objected to was Sir Nigel's power to curtail her freedom. It would be good to get back to London and take up Gail's job offer. Naturally, Charlie hadn't told her either of her Uncles about that.

3.

Magic Stevo and Stormy were going down well. Pup was almost on autopilot, which he sensed might be a warning sign to him that it was time to shake up his act. Then again, 'if it ain't broke don't fix it' and his act had never been better received. The table magic had wowed them and Stormy's interruptions from the stage had kept them laughing. They were now re-united on the stage and Stormy had challenged him to make a glamorous woman with a lot of cleavage, on the host's table, disappear into Stormy's dressing room. Then Stormy challenged him to do some mind reading:

'OK' said Pup, 'You've never seen me before, have you, Stormy?'

'No, Stevo'

Not long to go. After the mind reading with Stormy for laughs there's mind reading with audience members for effect, then the one big illusion and then the big finish with Stormy's joke. Seven minutes left. Not long now to him seeing Charlie at the Globe. Pup thought he needed a serious telling off as he was behaving like an adolescent. He was a mature, too mature, happily married man who couldn't help himself. He heard himself saying to Stormy:

'What the heck do you call this act?'

'The Aristocrats' said Stormy

Laughter, loud applause, whistles and, now they're standing. 'We did it again, Stormy', thought Pup. As Stormy and Magic Stevo take their bow, Pup notices a wealthy looking, elderly, black suited, silver haired, rimless glasses wearing, businessman enter the room – it was Nick Burgess.

4.

The next day, Pup was the last to arrive at the Euston Flyer. Dave, Nick and Scalesy were standing at one of the high circular tables in front of the big screen watching Sky Sports News. Nick looked like a fish out of water in the pub. He no longer went into pubs – he preferred hotel bars and clubs. It was business class, or preferably first class, all the way for Nick.

Scalesy, Dave and Pup were all pub-goers, although not as regularly as when the Chamberpots were playing cricket together. Then the Chequers, Spoons and The White Horse would see them most days each week and their lifelong friendships were forged. The Euston Flyer was spacious but so diverse in its punters and so noisy that there was no chance of their looking out of place or of their conversations being overheard.

'Anyone want a top up', said Pup as he approached them. They didn't, so Pup bought a Coke when what he really wanted was a pint of Golden Endeavour. He re-joined them. He knew that Nick would not have told Dave and Scalesy what he told Pup a hundred feet above Kensington High Street yesterday. It had shocked Pup that Nick was being asked to steal databases. This was far more dangerous than informing Chris of the travel arrangements of the ten targets on the team list. Nevertheless, there seemed to be a good chance that if Chris was getting Nick to do things he didn't want to do, then he was doing the same with the others.

It'd be interesting and hopefully, revealing, to see how Dave handled the tensions amongst them. Dave had called the meeting. This was the first time in the history of the Chamberpots that Dave had called a meeting and he'd only invited Scalesy, Nick and Pup. Pup expected the unexpected and after a 'Cheers' and clinking of glasses Dave launched right into it.

'I'm not exactly sure what is on Chris's bucket list or the big finale he's planning. I do know more than the three of you but I suspect that I don't know everything you've been asked to do. I reckon that fat cow Trude knows more than she's letting on. Would I be right in saying that you've all been asked to do more than he's ever asked you to do before?'

Dave looked at each one in turn with his showbizzy smile– it looked as if he was telling a joke. They each nodded.

'It's the same for me', continued Dave, 'and I'm doing a lot of meetings for Chris. I don't need to go into it all but it's at a level we've never been to before – it feels like more than just citizen journalism. It involves harming the establishment and we've never done that. It involves the London Olympics. It involves explosives, contract killers and drugs. For example, why did he get me to seek out the old landlord of Spoons? Think of a hobby he had?'

'He was a thieving bastard; he used to pour cheap spirits into the branded optics' said Nick

'Snakes and spiders' said Pup

'Correct. Snakes and spiders kill people' said Dave, 'So, this is new and dangerous. I'm not going to let Chris do anything that leads to me having a ruddy shit time after he's gone. I'm proposing that you all tell me what he's asking you to do. I can then put the pieces of the jigsaw together. I know Chris's ruddy, warped mind. I'll stop him and protect us. That's it. Sup up. Think about it. If you have anything to tell me I'm at the Institute of Directors, 116 Pall Mall, in the Morning Room, Thursday, every week from 2.30 to 4.30 – just ask for me at reception. No jeans and a jacket is required. Sithee at the Globe.'

Dave walked out of the Euston Flyer. Pup poured the substantial remains of Dave's beer into his own glass, looked at the other two and said, 'No Way'.

CHAPTER SEVEN: Men in women's clothing

Allegiance: loyalty to a person, cause or group

1.

CHARLIE HAD TRUDE'S PLACE and Steph had Chris's at the Chamberpots get-together at the Globe. Trude's mother, Pat, was very poorly and so Trude had given her apologies to Dave and Steph. As Steph and Charlie were the only two travelling from the North, Steph had arranged to meet Charlie at St Pancras before sharing a taxi to the Globe theatre.

This was Steph's idea as she thought it would help the success of the evening if she warned off Charlie about asking questions regarding current Chamberpot activities. They were all to meet at 6 for pre-theatre food and drinks at the Founders Arms on the Thames. It was 4.35 when Charlie and Steph found a table at Starbucks in St Pancras.

Steph found it hard to start a conversation as Charlie was constantly texting or saying 'Sorry, do you mind if I take this one' and walking off to take the call outside. Finally, there seemed to be a 'window of opportunity', to use a term Charlie used.

'I've a favour to ask you Charlie?' said Steph placing her hand gently on Charlie's arm.

'Oh please, Steph. You don't want me to give them the third degree like I did last time. Right?'

Steph nodded and smiled.

'That's cool. Dave gave me a bit of a slapped wrist, on the train journey back. I was only curious. Uncle Dave answered my questions. I was never going to blow it for you guys. I really was just curious as to what your little gang has been up to all these years'.

'Thanks Charlie – appreciate it. Dave and you seem to be getting on well – how's the job going?'

'It's nearly gone, Steph'

'Why's that?'

'Well, I think sports promotion and being a Commercial Director of a sports club could have worked for me but only if it was in a major City such as London, Manchester, Paris, Madrid, Milan and Munich.'

'So, have you got another position, Charlie?'

'I've got a pretty cool interim project, which will bring me back to London. My best friend, Gail, has her own PR Company and top Speakers Agency and she's expecting. I've kept doing some media work since giving up tennis so I know many in her network. She wants to be very part time for the first couple of years so the deal is I'll front it as CEO. Profit share, everything. Gail is very high profile. Me as the new Gail should lead to all sorts. I'm so lucky – well, business wise – not so much on the personal front. I'm crap at that.'

'Congratulations, Charlie'

'And before I start, I'm having a week in the sun. Dave is sending me out to see Chris in Malta – so that's exciting too.'

For a moment Steph's smile froze. She was speechless. She felt a prickly heat rising from the top of her chest to her throat and cheeks.

'Great. Let me know when you're going. I must give you something to take for Chris.'

2.

Steph felt hollow inside as if everything had been scooped out. She was queuing at the bar in the courtyard of the Globe Theatre. She'd offered to get the drinks to take in for the first half of the play. The others were close by to help her and she was half listening to Scalesy and Tricks in case they mentioned her name or asked her opinion about Chris. It didn't seem right coming to the Globe Theatre, home of the original Lord Chamberlain's Men, to see Shakespeare, without Chris. Then there was Charlie's bombshell about visiting Chris.

Combined, it had given her, a strong feeling, a feeling that was infrequent now, that she must still love Chris. But to what end? She felt consumed by nothingness.

Steph could see her hand on top of Chris's, black on white, as they marvelled, transfixed by the brilliant Mark Rylance as Johnny Rooster in Jerusalem. They'd seen him in Endgame too. Becket was above Shakespeare in Chris's 'all-time favourite' playwrights. In just a few minutes she'd be seeing the Rylance magic again as he played Richard III. Maybe she should go to Malta to see Chris. They could go to the lavish Manoel Theatre in Valletta. An 18th century theatre would be perfect to listen to some Baroque music or some Opera. Just to hold hands and press arms and shoulders together in the dark of a theatre audience, entranced by the music, would be bliss.

But No, that would waste nearly a year of her willpower. If she were with him she may find out what he was going to do. If she knew, then she would have to tell. She must do nothing to encourage their relationship. Chris must die as he wants to die, doing what he wants to do. Steph felt she must get used to this hollowness as it might remain for the rest of her life. 'I must work. I will love my independence – I will' she told herself unbelievingly.

Steph, naturally, hadn't told Pup of her reservations about his 'great idea' for a Chamberpots get-together at the Globe as a tribute to their leader. It was sweet of him and he'd even got seats for them all, in two boxes, on the stage. So, it meant a restricted view, but they'd be part of the action. It was a real treat and Steph told herself to relax and enjoy, but she felt nothing.

'Come back to us Steph', Pup had noticed Steph's frozen smile and faraway expression, 'Did you ever come here with Skip, I mean, Chris?'

'Oh. No-never .... We talked about it many times but just never got around to it. It's cool. Our seats look fabulous Pup – it's surreal. I can't wait to see Jonny Flynn as a woman too. He was in Jerusalem. He's a star'

'I think they all are Steph – and you are too. Oh no, that Old Dog, Dave's at it again. Can you hear him – here we go?'

'Don't you fucking dare, Dave' said Tricks

'Did I ever tell you that I was Buckingham to Chris's Richard at school? The great monologue is not Richard's but Buckingham's conning the court that he is persuading Richard to be King' said Dave

'Don't you dare fucking do it again, Dave. It's not funny' repeated Tricks.

Taking that as his cue, Dave jumped onto an empty barrel, and to the embarrassment of his fellow Chamberpots and the amusement of the standing and queuing crowds hammered his sickly smiling way through:

> Then know, it is your fault that you resign
> The supreme seat, the throne majestical,
> The scepter'd office of your ancestors,
> Your state of fortune and your due of birth,
> The lineal glory of your royal house,
> To the corruption of a blemished stock:
> Whilst, in the mildness of your sleepy thoughts,
> Which here we waken to our country's good,
> This noble isle doth want her proper limbs;
> Her face defaced with scars of infamy,
> Her royal stock graft with ignoble plants,
> And almost shoulder'd in the swallowing gulf
> Of blind forgetfulness and dark oblivion.
> Which to recure, we heartily solicit
> Your gracious self to take on you the charge
> And kingly government of this your land,
> Not as protector, steward, substitute,
> Or lowly factor for another's gain;
> But as successively from blood to blood,
> Your right of birth, your empery, your own.
> For this, consorted with the citizens,
> Your very worshipful and loving friends,
> And by their vehement instigation,
> In this just suit come I to move your grace.'

As the audience applauded Dave took the most extravagant of bows. Steph smiled but still felt the same. She'd seen that act before and Dave was a racist.

Steph thought back to the pre-theatre meal at the full and noisy Founders Arms pub. It hadn't been full of the usual Chamberpots banter and fun. Nick had phoned Pup to apologise that he couldn't make it, as he had to deal with a crisis at work. Too late for Pup to get a replacement and Tricks, especially, was very angry on Pup's behalf. Tricks was as quiet and well dressed as he'd been for the O2 tennis but he couldn't stop himself uttering a string of expletives about Nick.

But the flat atmosphere was not caused by Nick letting them down. Steph blamed Dave for it. Dave was his normal wisecracking self but it was his inviting Charlie, for a second time, which had changed the whole dynamic of the regular get-together of old friends.

Steph felt that Charlie was as uncomfortable being with the Chamberpots as she, Scalesy and Tricks were being with her. Perhaps Charlie was slightly intimidated, under her confident exterior, by their camaraderie. Maybe, she was slightly embarrassed that she'd accepted Dave's invitations because the events were too good to miss, even though she wasn't at all keen being with a bunch of oldies in her leisure hours.

Steph had noted, and Trude would have commented, that Pup and Tricks were both trying to impress Charlie with their wit and wisdom. Two men attracted by a high profile, attractive, young woman. The three of them even shared some contacts in the sports, media and entertainment worlds. Steph reflected that it was natural they'd be drawn together but it had the effect of splitting the table conversation. Steph thought Pup was trying too hard. He stood no chance of getting inside Charlie's knickers.

Steph recognised that she was to blame for the get-together having a faltering start as she hadn't been able to resist saying: 'Did you guys know that Dave is sending Charlie to see Chris?'

Scalesy, Tricks and Pup had known Dave and Chris a lot longer than Steph and so were shocked by this news. It seemed totally out of character for Chris and against all the principles and values of the Chamberpots. Nick and Trude would feel the same.

As worrying, this news proved that Dave knew far more than the other Chamberpots about what Chris was intending. As one, they felt betrayed, excluded and afraid of Dave and Chris.

Charlie didn't say anything, but looked at Dave, when Steph posed the question to Scalesy, Pup and Tricks. Dave came in immediately and smilingly:

'No worries. It was Chris's idea. This is nothing to do with us. A company he knows has come up with an online sports game that he wants to launch at the Olympics. He needs someone to launch it, with all the right media contacts and I know no-one better than Charlie. It might be a laugh for both, which reminds me I haven't told you my Christmas joke.'

Steph could sense that Dave had nipped it in the bud. The conversation couldn't go anywhere, particularly in front of Charlie. There was no alternative but to listen to Dave's joke.

'On Christmas Day there was a ventriloquist, a plumber and a wrestler killed in a multiple car pile-up on the M1. Now that's sad but the good news is that they all went to heaven.

St Peter, at the Gates, said: 'Before I can let you in I just have to check you've all still got your wits about you. What I'd like you all to do is give me one thing that you have with you that reminds us all of Christmas. Who'll go first?'

The ventriloquist talked to himself for a minute and then took out of his pocket a lighter. He lit it, pointed to the flame and said, 'It's a candle'.

St Peter said, 'Well done. Come on in'

Next to go was the plumber. He was used to making things up, particularly exorbitant prices of plumbing jobs, so was ready and took out of his belt buckle a large bunch of keys. He gently rattled the keys together and said 'They're sleigh bells'.

'Wonderful', said St Peter, 'Welcome'.

The wrestler had been thinking hard while the other two had their go. He was ready. He slapped his biceps, mimed a knife edge chop and shouted 'Bring It On! Wooooooooo!!!!!'. He then took out of his pocket a bra and a thong – which he waved under St Peter's nose.

St Peter looked aghast; understandably as they'd had enough of sex scandals in the church, and angrily said 'What's the meaning of this?'

To which the wrestler said, 'They're Carol's'

Steph allowed herself a smirk now and recognised how adept Dave was at changing the subject. Now, though, she wasn't thinking about Malta. She was in her seat listening to Elizabethan music being played on Elizabethan instruments in the balcony next to her. On the stage, in full view of the audience, the actors, the players, were readying themselves for the performance. Closest to the stage were the standing audience, drinks and food in hand and behind them layer upon layer of the seated audience – the posh lot.

The Globe was exactly as it was 400 years ago. The actors were joking with each other and the audience. The buzz in the audience was loud and expectant. There was a fanfare from the musicians. Then almost without anyone noticing, Mark Rylance as Richard, in black, ordinary looking, shuffled on at the back, stage left to the audience. He was to the right, only just visible, of Steph. Steph thought how photogenic he was. How surprising he'd not made it big in the movies but he will. Rylance as Richard said, quietly and, conversationally, to the audience:

'Now is the winter of our discontent
Made glorious by this sun of York ......

3.

Chris was angry at his incompetence. He was in Upper Barrakka Gardens, again, in Valletta. He was on his second mini bottle of Red

Label red wine. It was 10 a.m. After one more mini bottle he would walk down the hill and visit St Johns Co- Cathedral to view his two all-time favourite paintings by Caravaggio. He was looking at his action list for today. He thought it was pathetic that he couldn't remember the list.

He'd just told the outside bar owner to ensure that he always took the money from Chris for his wine purchases on a pay as you go basis. Last week he'd walked off, yet again, without paying his bill. He could never remember whether he'd paid his bill or not but was too ashamed to ask. He was happy to act crazy but not to be crazy. His cinematic long-term memory was annoying him just as much as his lack of short-term memory. For days now, he'd seen himself walking back from junior school, in his grey woolly jumper, that his Mum had knitted. He wore a grey shirt, yellow and green tie too. When he arrived home, he opened the back door and saw his Dad slapping his Mum hard on the side of her face. He wanted this memory to disappear but it just kept coming back.

Chris was preparing for the visit of Charlie. He'd surprised himself by finding his 'to do' list neatly folded in his sunglasses case.

He had a list of what he'd last said to people. He'd transferred to his 'to do' list what he'd last said to the people he was to meet today. He was embarrassed about how many times a day he repeated himself. The only saving grace was that before the operation he'd have shouted, because of his poor hearing, the repeated statement or question. At least the poor sod he was with only had to read a few words. Still, by listing what he thought he'd said immediately after a meeting it gave him a chance that he'd be less confusing the next time they met. Confusing those helping him with his final solution just wouldn't do.

Next Chris took out of his bag a dark red plastic wallet folder. Inside were letters, post it notes and press cuttings neatly stapled together. 3 of the A4 brown envelopes had a single letter on the front of each. The letters were T, N and D. Chris could hardly believe that he now had to keep records of the Chamberpots guilty secrets. He scolded himself that he must remember to copy these files, so that he had a backup should he lose his bag. After all, he thought, 'Every puppet master must know which strings to pull.'

He opened the 'N' envelope and took out of it a cutting reporting the inquest on the death of Rosie Charlton. On the report were scribbled 'RK' & a mobile phone number.

He was about to meet the journalist, Pete Bryan, that made the report. He would get Pete Bryan to ring Nick Burgess to say he was about to publish new information he had on the suicide of Rosie Charlton.

Pete Bryan would then call Richard King to tell him that Nick was willing to do as he requested. Nick and the leaders in the Supramax global network would then persuade the Supramax Founders to make the changes to the marketing plan. Richard King would become even wealthier and as part of the overall deal would give Chris access to millions of computers and smartphones, through lines of sponsorship in the $100 billion direct selling industry.

4.

Nick Burgess was meeting with Richard King at Berlin airport, while most of the Chamberpots were at the Globe theatre. He was ice cold. He didn't know what would happen next but he knew this was a turning point. None of the roads ahead looked inviting and Richard King was twiddling his bracelet and not making eye contact again.

Nick had been a national or regional director for US global, multi-level marketing companies for over thirty years. Multi-level marketing was often called network marketing or referral marketing. It was big business now – every famous name in the States was involved Trump, Gates, Buffet, Tracy, Robbins, Rohn, Covey - the list of advocates is endless. Amway and Herbalife are the best known, largest and longest established but there were many relative newcomers, like Supramax, which followed the same model.

Averting bad publicity and covering up some of the unfortunate, and in the case of Rosie Charlton, sad incidents were an essential part of Nick's job. 8 out of 10 independent business owners wouldn't make any money and will leave each year to be replaced by another cohort. Very few are winners but Nick didn't like to call the rest losers, like the leaders of lines of sponsorship did. Although there is no risk to these people of losses if they follow their company's guidance many of them follow their sponsor's advice which can lead to loss and stress. The multi-level marketing company makes its money out of product sales, mainly to the independent business owners and low-priced starter kits.

The independent business owners' leadership make some money out of bonuses on product sales of their network with much more money coming from events, seminars and a whole raft of support tools they produce for the independent business owners. The pursuit of the American dream can become a nightmare. Rosie Charlton was one who couldn't find a way out of the nightmare. .

Rosie Charlton had been persuaded by her up line to invest in down line members of her group, and buy stock to qualify her for a leadership position. This cost a lot of money and the earnings from commissions and bonuses were small. As costly, is investing in looking prosperous like a winner should. More expense was accumulated from the learning media she bought and the travel to and tickets to events she paid for.

It was all done, Nick rationalised, as they wanted to buy their way to a senior position in the network where they expected to become rich. It was their guilty secret from the company that they had received bonuses on stock they'd bought that they hadn't any customers for.

Nick thought these people were greedy and gullible. The company always made it clear it was not a get rich quick scheme and they should start part time with little expenditure. It was greed and gullibility that made the top leaders, like Richard King, rich and so Nick turned a blind eye to what was going on in the lower levels of leadership.

Rosie Charlton had got to the leadership level which allowed her to participate in the network's earning from ticket sales from meetings, seminars, rallies, family re-unions and from the sale of motivational media. Rosie, like others before her and others after her, lost her home, family, friends and mind to her business. She could see no way out and had wanted to end it all.

After two minutes, it felt like two hours to Nick, silence Richard King spoke: 'I'm sorry Nick, this won't do. You only have one week left to get us all a meeting with the founders to agree the changes. Don't be a sacrificial lamb Nick. It was assisted suicide and you know the journalist knows who supplied the pills. They'll hang you out to dry.'

ACT THREE: AUGUST 2012

CHAPTER EIGHT: Where the Elite Meet to Eat

Hacker. Someone who seeks to breach defences and exploit weaknesses in a computer system or network.

1.

'LOOK AT SIR JIMMY he was a mate of yours, wasn't he Dave? One moment they're lining the streets of Leeds and Scarborough, celebrating him as a hero and the next hundreds and hundreds of people are coming forward to testify against him as a paedophile, rapist and the rest. Look at Lance Armstrong, maybe he's more protected by the elite, but I bet you it won't be long before more guilty secrets are revealed.

Once people think they can dish the dirt – they love it and there's the compensation too. Anyway, if Chris is found to be behind something illegal, the spotlight will swing over to us as well. Everyone that might have wanted to have a go at any of us will do so. Chris can destroy us all.'

Nick was talking as he walked around the Wimbledon complex, with Dave. They had Number One Court tickets for the tennis at the Olympics.

Wimbledon had been transformed into the Olympics, corporate colours of purple and white lettering with the major sponsors branding. Every Olympic venue looked the same and sold the same refreshments and merchandise. Dave had already been annoyed that he couldn't find anywhere to smoke and then hadn't been able to get 'a real beer in my own ruddy country'.

Nick wasn't much aware of his surroundings; he was getting straight to the point with Dave. Nick wanted Dave to hasten Chris's demise.

2.

Next day Dave was in St James Park, Newcastle to watch the Men's Football in the Olympics. Super kid Neymar, he of the swerving shots, overhead kicks, mazy dribbles and blistering speed was playing. It's always the speed that frightens defenders. Dave thought black players were high risk at international level because they were 'moody, lazy bastards'. Oscar was in the side too, pulling the midfield strings. Dave guessed that most of the Brazil side for the 2014 World Cup were on display. He was angry again. He'd walked up what seemed a million stairs to reach the very top of the stand. He was gasping for breath, the fags clearly influenced his lung capacity and he realised Tricks and Trude were fitter than he was. He'd thought himself fit. Then when they got to the bar he found they were serving 'the same old ruddy piss' that was at Wimbledon.

Dave wondered if Tricks secretly liked being the focus of attention, when they were out together. The Woooooooo!!!!! and people shouting, 'Hey Rick' at him, even the occasional autograph hunter and not just kids either, men and women nearly Tricks' age. Tricks was the only one at the ground in an Armani suit with a Rolex.

'Will this game be fixed Tricks?' asked Trude.

'No way of knowing – must be a chance but I don't know, Trude. It's what they'll fix – for example Brazil to win by just one goal or to score a penalty in the second half. There are so many events at the Olympics too. Some of what they fix will be what's easiest and high profile enough to get a lot of money riding on it. What's easiest will be a match official or a goalkeeper that'll take a bribe. Most illegal gambling is co-ordinated from India, so that's where the big money is made - an India v Pakistan one-day game of cricket will have $250 million illegally bet on it.

'So, are football and cricket more likely to be fixed than, say, tennis?' asked Trude.

'Yeah, I guess so, tennis also has the best anti-cheat technology and reviews like American Football, but every sport has cheats. There are always tennis players and umpires being investigated and legal betting being suspended because of swings. There's a market for everything and every market can be fixed. Even who is going to win a political election, or come second or third. The bigger the event being televised around the world the more illegal gambling there is so the more cheating goes on. They'll have been working on the Olympics from years back.

Anywhere there's a programme of drug use is vulnerable. Where there are drugs there are athletes, coaches and officials with something to hide who will make deals. It's different with the Olympics though because the fixing, say use of drugs, will be a national system for that sport. Millions will have been spent to be one step ahead of the testing regime. It's only well after the medals have been dished out that the testing regime will catch up with what happened.'

'You're an expert Tricks. Should we run a book on which Olympics events are rigged, then?' joked Trude, 'What would you go for?'

'I'd go for field events, then the marathon but cycling and boxing will have fixes in there – not for the winners, necessarily, but look at the results of some of the lower places or the number of no jumps. But maybe there's something rigged in all of them. It's the biggest show in the world and everyone knows the IOC is corrupt. The networks will have been planning this for years. They'll bet on anything even the length of a game. Even injury or floodlight failure can be fixed. It's clever stuff but it shouldn't spoil your enjoyment as nearly all the athletics and swimming winners will be the very best there is in that event. I reckon wrestling as sports entertainment is more honest - the winner and the finishing move is agreed in advance and everyone knows we take drugs. Mind you, people still bet on pro wrestling even though it's just a show. Crazy world' said Tricks.

'Mum never really recovered from the spot fixing in cricket. It took the edge off everything for her - county games – the lot' Trude said quietly.

'So sorry about Pat, Trude' said Tricks

'No need to be Tricks', Trude brightened, 'She was, sort of, ready for it and she wasn't in pain, which was her biggest fear. She went downhill so quickly that – well she just knew. No famous last words either, after they'd taken off all the bits and pieces she just was holding my hand, and whispered 'Thanks precious'. Pat drifted away as quietly as someone tossing away a chiffon scarf. It wouldn't be me tossing it away because I ain't got a chiffon scarf. There was no drama, for once in her life. Anyway, we had the most fantastic knees up, a real celebration – after the funeral. It seemed like all the sports fans of Yorkshire were there. It cost a fortune but what a party. Steph came.'

'Do you think that Steph's in touch with Chris?' the ever-smiling Dave, interrupted.

'Oh, I'm sure she will be,' said Trude, 'Before you ask me, no I don't know Chris's plans. I haven't heard from him'.

'Now would I ask you both to this fabulous match, courtesy of Chris sending us the tickets, to talk about the Chamberpots. No and thrice No. When you're all at the athletics I'll be with Chris in Malta and I'm happy to take any messages from you both.' smiled Dave.

'I bet you would Dave and you'd have the envelope steamed open and the contents read, before handing anything over.' Trude said matter of factly. they'd known each other for a very long time.

'And I'd tell you I'd done it too. I call a spade a ruddy shovel, as well you know' said Dave.

Tricks put a heavily muscled arm on both of Dave's shoulders. His eyes were now only inches away from Dave's. Both Trude and Dave expected the next move would be a head butt and blood spurting from Dave's forehead.

Instead, Tricks said very calmly and quietly, 'I've got a message for Chris. After the athletics, that's me out of the Chamberpots. I cannot stand Nick and you're fucking around with us, Dave. You've messed up our days out by involving your niece in them. I don't know what you've been up to in London for Chris and I don't give a fuck – I'm out, mate. Sorry Trude, but I've thought long and hard since the Globe. Chris has never been the bravest leader in the world and Dave, my little Northern buddy, you're no hero either. So, whatever you're both up to I think it likely that you're about to run out of luck. If any one of the Chamberpots get hurt by your little scheme I will take responsibility for finding a man who will enjoy crushing your balls. Let's watch the game, have a few beers and talk about the times together that we did enjoy.'

Dave, Trude and Tricks took their seats in the stand – in that order. Something was very different about this than all the other football matches they'd watched together in the past. Most of the capacity crowd of so many nationalities weren't fans of either side. So, there was no chanting and singing. But it was friendly and happy, just different. The Chamberpots were different now and unhappy.

3.

Pup put six postcards of Malta scenes into an envelope and then into his back pocket. He greeted the returning Charlie. He gave her his brightest, hopefully not cheesy, smile and said: 'So how was, Chris?'

'No idea!' said Charlie. 'We didn't meet up. It was lucky that I was there on business and that he wasn't an important part of my itinerary or I would be pissed with him.'

'I don't understand. How did you get the postcards?' said Pup

'He was too ill to meet me. The recording said that.'

'Have you got a recording?'

'No – just the postcards. Let me explain,' said Charlie. 'It was all a bit cloak and dagger. When I got to Valetta and St John's Co-Cathedral - at exactly the right time. I know that's unusual for me, I was met by a bloke in a uniform. He said something like 'Mr. Hastings apologises for not being here' and then gave me one of those headsets that tell you about the place and a leaflet with a map of where in the cathedral the different bits of the audio are. They're marked by numbers. Anyway, when I left the same guy took the headset back from me and gave me the envelope. What's with you and Chris and the postcards?'

'You looked?' exclaimed Pup.

'As you would too,' said Charlie.

'Aw Chris always sent me six or so postcards from everywhere he's travelled in the world. It's his way of saying he cares. Was there any message for anyone on the recording - something for Trude or Steph? asked Pup.

'No, the voice on the recording was of an Italian woman. I'd been told to go to the oratory and then press the number on the leaflet to hear the recording. I did that and her voice said that Mr. Hastings was ill but please look at the Caravaggio.'

'Which one – there are two?'

'The famous one, of course.' said Charlie; 'it's the huge one of the be-heading. The voice said that it was Mr. Hastings' favourite painting. I can see why Caravaggio is a genius even though he was a murdering so-and-so. He certainly does violent death well on canvas too. The voice said something like the painting looked more like a theatrical performance than a religious scene. The red of the cloak coming out of the gloomy starkness of the background is what everyone remembers. The voice apologised for Chris not being there and he may never be well enough to see the great Caravaggio again. The voice said that this Caravaggio was the only one that is signed – in the blood, I think.'

Charlie didn't say to Pup that the voice on the headset had told her that her father and Sir Nigel's retirement years would only be pleasant if information about a sordid affair was kept quiet. A reason was provided for Charlie to work with Pup to help the Lord Chamberlain's Men and their projects. This reason was that her Uncle Dave was a loose cannon capable of destroying all around him that may know his guilty secret.

4.

Chris is writing in the leather-bound book to Steph:

123

So, you're at the end of this lovely book and you will have heard about the end of me. If the technology worked then you'll have found out about my little accident. I can assure you I'm no hero and the little pills I took will have ensured my demise was quick and painless.

I'm laughing as I'm writing this because I feel like Cyrano De Bergerac writing all those love letters from the battlefield to Roxane. You are my Roxane, Steph, but thankfully, he says, blushing, unlike Cyrano I was lucky enough to consummate the love and we haven't had a 14-year gap of pretending to be somebody that we're not. We've just had just eighteen months of that.

My guilty secret from you is that some months ago I did come back to London and even had time in York. I wanted to see you, of course, but I was incognito as I was checking out the security arrangements for someone visiting Malta. I wore Dave's 'costume' of blazer, tie and grey trousers. In posh hotels and clubs, you become invisible and can go anywhere. You wouldn't have recognised me -lol.

I hope that I have left a legacy that will do a tiny sliver of good for the world. It should do. Once the technology, big data and motivation to use it is in place then it's like an ever-growing tsunami that can't be stopped.

The reason hundreds of thousands will play my game around the world is greed through the addiction that is gambling – when the fun stops – stop. Gaming is the gift to Malta that keeps on giving and all I've done is duplicate the Malta model for the dark, unlicensed net. In many years' time they'll remember me as a disruptive entrepreneur rather than the bringer down of corrupt folk in power.

Once GCHQ have found out what I've done then you'll be relieved to know that there is nothing that could have been gained by you telling your bosses earlier about the Lord Chamberlain's Men or me. The Chamberpots and I have never done any physical harm to any of the crooks that are leading our various countries and corporations around the world.

In my defence, unleashing the dark web and the Internet of things so that many devices will collect and transmit data about the habits, behaviour and corruption that these leaders do daily is no more than the CIA and GCHQ do daily too. It is no more than Google do and I got the idea from Blackrock's Aladdin computers that inform the great Gods' Goldman Sachs and JP Morgan who in turn control the world's governments and money supply. The best bit is that I've found a way to replace some of the baddies with some of the goodies.

So, there is nothing you could have done and there is absolutely nothing that your bosses could or would have done to stop me. We were never a risk to national security. There are hackers working for government and large corporations and there are hackers not working for government and large corporations and I chose to work with them to try and make the world a better governed place. It all works by AI, robotics and machine learning. Feed in the data and the accuracy of prediction of behaviour is better than any human can do. It's why cancer and the cure will all be by machine — it never makes mistakes and improves every time. Even translation is a third more accurate by machine than professional linguists.

Steph, please will you help me now I'm no longer here? There are a few things I must tell you so that the authorities can protect some people that I am no longer able to. You've met Charlie and of course Pup you've known for ages. I'm very fond of both for very different reasons and I can tell you it took a massive effort on my part not to see Charlie, who I've never met in person, when she came to Malta. I admire them both as they are the future and I believe their energy and ambition might continue to keep the work of the Lord Chamberlain's men going. This would be in entirely their own way, perhaps even through politics or philanthropy or a movement. They have the brains and courage to do it.

Before Geoff, Pup's father, died he told me and Pup some things about Dave and Charlie's father that you also now need to know so that you can tell the appropriate authorities. Dave was a great friend of mine from school but I now know him to be vile and without principle when he sees that there is money to be made. He's a bigot and a racist too — we'll never forgive him for that joke he made about what colour our children might be.

Dave's guilty secret is that he has committed crimes that should have seen him behind bars for most of his life. He is lucky that the establishment closed ranks to protect him and save their own skins. Dave doesn't know that Geoff has told Pup but if the secret looks like appearing in the public domain, Pup's life and anyone he is associated with, for example, Charlie, is threatened.

Dave is a very lucky man but one day his luck will run out. The current inquiries and police investigations into historical sex abuse are closing in around Dave. He is going to leave the country and with a new identity. You don't need to know the details but, back in the day, Dave who would do and did do anything he could to supplement his paltry teacher's income, was a fixer for a sex ring and paedophile club.

As is now common knowledge these clubs used orphans in various institutions, but mainly in Northern Ireland. A handful of club members used to fly out to Belfast airport quite regularly for a week-end's entertainment. At the airport, they would be greeted by Dave, who had made all the arrangements.

One of the frequent flyers was Sir Nick's brother and Charlie's 'father'. Geoff was not involved in the club or ring but some of the financial transactions he was making on behalf of his clients aroused his suspicion. His suspicions were confirmed when there was a substantial pay-out that he found was for a cover-up. There had been an 'accident' that occurred with one of the young girls. The money was routed through Dave's personal account, which is how Geoff found out about Dave's involvement.

The cover-up protected Dave from spending his life in prison but at that point Geoff ditched his seedy, wealthy clients and, although few of the Lord Chamberlain's men ever noticed it, Dave and Geoff hardly ever spoke again. Dave is a vile man - great company but a vile man. One of the reasons that Lord Chamberlain's men stick together – well, at least to meet a few times a year and provide information to me is that I know their guilty secrets.

So, Steph, I don't want to burden you with anything else but if you could just ensure the safety from Dave, of Pup and Charlie, by a word in the appropriate ears it would be really appreciated. I'm sorry that I can't show my appreciation in person.

I thought I'd leave you on a more cheerful note:

Jack was about to marry Jill and his father took him to one side.

'When I married your Mother, the first thing I did when we got home was take off my trousers,' he said. 'I gave them to your Mother and told her to put them on. When she did, they were enormous and she said to me that she couldn't possibly wear them as they were too large.

I told her, 'of course they're too big. I wear the trousers in this family and I always will. Ever since that day we have never had a single problem. Jack took his father's advice and as soon since he got Jill alone after the wedding, he did the same thing; took off his trousers, gave them to Jill and told her to put them on.

Jill said the trousers were too big and she couldn't possibly wear them. 'Exactly' replied Jack, 'I wear the trousers in this relationship and I always will. I don't want you to forget that.'

Jill paused and removed her knickers and gave them to Jack. 'Try these on,' she said, so he tried them on but they were too small. 'I can't possibly get into your knickers,' said Jack.

'Exactly,' replied Jill. 'And if you don't change your bloody attitude, you never will.'

And here's a poem of mine to remember me by. Hope you like it.

All Rather Colourful

The lights were red
My mind said go
My legs led
The road slowed
I streamed my thoughts
They gave no clue
Flying high
Tied up too
Accelerating quickly
Without moving an inch
Feeling so silly
At a pinch
The white line grew
Into a wall
I stared aghast
I'm not that tall
Quickly I flew
The wall smiled
It would do
I'm toast

My white coffin was carried
By ladies in green
My bride never married
Didn't seem bothered

The mourners in yellow
Were laughing aloud
A few could not bellow
Stuffing food

Some prayed for forgiveness
A few applauded my sins
The speeches were rubbish
Hadn't learned a thing
The grass was green
The earth was brown
The box went down
Nowt more to be seen

Sorry I wasn't the marrying kind, not again anyhow! You know I loved you. Love and hugs xxxx

5.

Tricks was texting on his iPhone with his back leaning against a pillar outside the Excel Arena. He wasn't looking forward to his afternoon at the Olympics wrestling as he had little interest in amateur wrestling. As he texts every few minutes someone would shout at him 'its Ric Flair', or 'What's up nature boy?' or 'wooo' to which he nodded without making eye contact. Sometimes, he showed four fingers, palm in. This signalled the four horsemen.

Tricks was feeling sorry for himself. Of all the Chamberpots he was closest to the underworld and so he got all the worst jobs from Chris and Dave. To be fair to Chris and Dave he hadn't been called on many times to do anything more than provide information on targets. Now that Chris was in Malta and Dave was doing the asking the tasks were more dangerous. Tricks was always only one step away from either prison or the gutter. The gutter was more likely if his wealthy clients felt he was under investigation.

Tricks suspected Dave knew that Chris had bailed him out before by hiring a team to show that heroin found in his gym had been planted. It was still no reason for smiley Dave to treat him like a lackey. Showing his contempt for Dave in front of the other Chamberpots hadn't been a good idea. It was now a race between him and Dave as to who would get even first.

Tricks was waiting for Jez Hopkins to turn up. Jez, was a site manager, and van driver, for one of the major temporary structures contractors for the London Olympics. Jez had been working inside the Olympics security bubble for five months, mainly building temporary stands. He was well known to G4S and all the other security geeks and they all did favours for each other. If anyone could sneak a small box of gifts into a hospitality suite, with someone to hand the gifts out, it was Jez.

There was a tap on Tricks' left shoulder. He looked left and a voice from the right said, 'Got you there, Nature Boy, you're losing your touch'. It was Jez.

'And you're living dangerously, Jez. Rather unwise I think – especially for a midget!'

Jez was not that small, no more than six inches smaller than Tricks, and he was muscular, from working out at Tricks' and Spit's gym. The only thing spoiling Jez looking like a mini version of Tricks was a small bump protruding over his belt where a six pack should have been. He was wearing black from top to toe – t shirt, jeans and baseball cap.

'So, is this it?' said Jez pointing to a small 2012 Olympics ruck sack next to Tricks' left foot.

'Sure.' said Tricks, 'Open one of the boxes inside'.

Jez opened a gold box and inside was a small gold and silver-plated portable speaker. The speaker had the instantly recognizable 'Bose' trademark on it.

'Mmmmh nice', said Jez, 'Can I have one for doing the job?'.

'Thought you'd say that Jez, but take this one.' said Tricks handing Jez a large jiffy bag, and your fee is inside too. Mike will be outside Hendon Central tube at 5 am tomorrow morning for you to pick him up. He'll be easy to recognise as he'll be the only person on the street and he'll be dressed as a silver service waiter', smiled Tricks, enjoying his own joke.

'We'll want to check him out that he's not carrying anything. He can change into our clobber so he looks the same as the other guys in the van.' said Jez.

'Of course. The only thing he'll take with him into the hospitality suite is this bag of gifts and he's got all the staff clearances once he's in the Park – it was getting him in the Park, and next to the Hospitality suite, that was our problem. Thanks Jez.'

'OK bud, hey what's that new ring – one on each hand now?' said Jez spotting the two WWE Hall of Fame rings.

'Yeah. The real Ric got another one for the four horsemen in March. I've got to be the real deal you know – fans notice these things'.

6.

'Why are we meeting here?' Dave asked Chris. They were in Modica, Sicily at the Antica Dolceria Bonajuta eating cannelloni. Chris was wearing A Northampton Saints rugby shirt, buttoned at the top with collar up and a green baseball hat. Dave was in a short-sleeved white, formal shirt with a blue tie. It was a sweltering hot day. Chris answered by writing on a small notebook 'My favourite place – chocolate city. We can't be seen together in Malta.'

'I saw James a few weeks ago at an Old Boys golf day. He asked after his favourite right back. You were never as good at football as me. I was always surprised James picked you. Anyway, I told him you were dying in Malta.'

Chris wrote 'I was memorable at footie. How was James?'

'Dying of pancreatic cancer – I won't give him long by the look of him. He's loaded but no time to spend it. Anyway, he's a fat bastard now.'

Chris wrote 'What have you got for me, Old Dog?'

Dave handed Chris a memory stick.

Chris wrote, 'When you've finished here then walk that way' he pointed, 'along Coso Umberto until you see the Museo Cioccolatomodico. You like museums – it's only two rooms. In the room with the chocolate map a guy will give you a package - your new ID, passport, tickets, cards – the lot. You'll need it all for after our Saturday gig.'

CHAPTER NINE: Super Saturday

Stoical: Achieving happiness by accepting fate

1.

LAST NIGHT PUP HAD CALLED Charlie 'posh' on the phone. 'Posh' as in 'your posh friends'. As he said it, he knew it was a stupid, ruinous, thing to say. He'd only called her to check where they'd meet today. He'd been upset by how many people Charlie knew who were benefiting from the corporate hospitality at the Games but had absolutely no interest in the athletes.

Pup regarded most of these people as being the lapdogs of the corrupt Olympics hierarchy. His bias was that posh meant privileged and wealthy but it doesn't necessarily mean corrupt. Pup realised immediately that he was wrong to call Charlie 'posh'. He also realised how essential it was to Chris's plan that Charlie did know and socialise with these people to give them a free copy of the video game that Chris had been involved in producing. Charlie and he seemed to be getting on great since Charlie had been to Malta and Pup would say he was sorry as soon as they met.

Pup knew that his jibes at Charlie's network and upbringing were attention seeking. He was jealous. He had no right to be jealous but he wanted to be more attractive to her than her past and present lovers. Not that he could count himself her lover. In fact, he was scared stiff that she may suggest they spend a night together. He didn't fancy being compared to her past and present lovers. It might all go horribly wrong and be the end of his favourite fantasy.

Pup opened the door of Peak Performance gym. It was 5.30 on Saturday morning so there was only Tricks there. Tricks embraced him 'Good to see you Bud, thanks for getting here so early. Here's the tickets for everyone'

'Why can't you make it? It's going to be amazing.' said Pup

'I'm in a bit of trouble and there's something that won't wait that I need to take care of. Shame, I was looking forward to it too – especially as Old Dog and Nick aren't there. You'll get a massive price for these three tickets – they're like gold dust. Take Charlie to Vegas'

'No chance.', laughed Pup, 'By the way, I got your message to Skip. I sent him an Olympics postcard – he sends them to me.'

'What did you say?'

'I just said 'Thanks for the Olympics tickets. We'll miss you. All's well at home although the old dog is starting to smell really bad'

2.

Steph picked up her miniscule handbag and smoothed down her very short skirt as she announced she was going to 'the ladies.' Trude got up and gathered her own antithesis of Steph's handbag to her, trying to stop its contents spilling out as she followed Steph to the loo. She was aware that they made a strange pair, Steph, the epitome of style and poise, herself, well, a bit less so.

Trude wanted to be able to talk to Steph alone and the stereotype of ladies going together to the loo notwithstanding, she had to take this chance. As they emerged from the cubicles to stand at the wash basins in front of the mirror, Trude tried not to notice Steph's immaculate manicure and to banish the thought of those crimson nails raking down Chris's back, from her mind. She could see Chris's back from the small tattoo with the masks of comedy and tragedy below his neckline right down to the bottom of his spine. She was not jealous, but she was wistful.

'So, Chris hasn't had much to say.' Trude said as Steph applied a glossy layer of petal plum to her full lips. Trude had thought carefully about the words she used. She did not want to give the impression

134

that she had heard nothing, although she had not, but rather get Steph to reveal the details of any contact she had had with Chris. Steph's eyes met Trude's in the mirror as Steph pursed her lips to ensure an even spread of her lip gloss. She raised her eyebrows and her eyes widened slightly. Trude could not make out whether Steph's expression was quizzical or non-committal. She tried again.

'So, what do you hear from our glorious leader?' she laughed, but even so the sound was reedy and unconvincing. Steph had her face powder out now and was applying a shimmering layer of a delicately glittering substance to her high cheek bones. She wanted to know if Trude had heard from Chris but from the way Trude had spoken it didn't sound like it. She looked at the reflection of Trude's hands in the mirror, she had been washing them for as long as Steph had been touching up her make up.

She did not answer the question and instead said, 'Jessica Ennis is very impressive don't you think?'. Trude hesitated, before she blurted out, 'Oh yes, rather.' She felt backfooted, her hesitation had made it sound as though she did not know who Jessica Ennis was.

'Oh, Chris?' Steph said, as though Trude's question had only just registered.

'She was applying mascara now with a thin wand, making her already lush eyelashes appear even more prolific. 'You know what he's like, only ever gets in touch when he wants something.'

'Yes, he can be very self-absorbed.' Trude said. 'No news is good news where he is concerned!' she paused. 'So, you've not heard anything?'

'Not much, you?' Steph said.

Trude moved over to the hand dryer on the wall. 'So, you've heard something then, just not much?' Trude cringed, that had sounded weak, needy and Trude was neither.

Steph gave an elegant shrug, observed by Trude in the corner of the mirror.

'Well like we said, no news - you know how it is with him' She said.

'Oh yes, I certainly do!' Trude gave another hollow laugh.

This had been a mistake. It was far from her usual direct approach to everything, and she was sounding very back footed. Steph was clearly giving nothing away and she, Trude, had nothing to give away.

Sometimes, Trude thought, Chris caused way more frustration, speculation and concern than he deserved, and often she really resented him for it. Like now. Trying to regain her composure she swung out of the ladies' room leaving Steph making some final adjustments to her make up.

After a few steps, Trude stopped and took a postcard she'd received from Chris with a scene of Lampedusa in Italy. Trude read the message again, even though she knew every word by heart.

The message was: *'I'm not on this sad island of refugees but in my final refuge now. It's a happier place bar none be-cause our love never died. xxxx'*

Trude went back and poking her head around the door, with tears running down her cheeks, blurted out in a shaky voice to Steph, 'I can't cope with seeing them all at the Olympics Steph. Everything is too raw – tell them – they'll understand. I'm sorry.'

3.

Pup walked into the Pizza Express on the Euston Road. He was to meet Charlie there and then they'd take the Olympics train from St Pancras.

He spotted Charlie near the window. It looked as if she'd finished eating but whomever was with her had left most of their meal.

'Hi Charlie, first thing is I'm sorry for what I said about you having posh friends. I wasn't inferring anything about you and it's none of my business who you know or like. I'm sorry. Shall I have a coffee while you finish and settle up?'.

'No, Pup, we might as well go. Like, I only said to meet her so that you could meet my bessie friend and new business partner, Gail. Only you can't. She's gone'.

'Looks like Gail lost her appetite?'

'Nope she's gone to have a baby. She went to the loo and her waters broke. She texts me and I get her fellah, Mark, who works around the corner to get here pronto and whisk her off to hospital. He'll let me know when the new baby girl is born. It could be hours yet. Let's go. '

'Hell, Charlie, you're very calm about it. Didn't you want to with her?'

'Nope, three's a crowd and too many cooks and all that. It's probably my fault. I told Gail how we were getting on fine and Gail rolled her eyes at me mentioning another bloke in my life. She probably thought I had enough on my plate, including building her business, without you to cope with as well'.

'I'm surprised you were talking about me, Charlie'.

'Well, we weren't. There was no time before she needed the loo and I've told you the rest'

'But why say anything?'

'I wanted to ask her opinion on an old guy I think we could start promoting as a future leader of the opposition. I think he fits the person spec that Chris would like - values and principles – but the only downside is that he's boring and no-one outside Westminster and his constituency has heard of him'.

'Chris's money and you putting a promotional plan, a movement and a team together can easily fix that', said Pup.

'Yeah, it's worth a look – this guy might be the first good apple we find to replace the bad apples the Lord Chamberlain's Men have been chucking out of the barrel', said Charlie.

'What about asking your Uncle, Sir Nigel, a few questions?'

'That's a No-No. He's fiercely intelligent and too suspicious. I couldn't trust him.'

'Let me tell you a little story about trust, Charlie'.

'If you must, but make it quick'

'Skip, I mean Chris, has been going to Malta for years from way before his cancer op. He loves it there because of 'trust'. He told me the story of a man coming into the bar and asking the barman if he knew Chris Hastings. The barman said, 'Everyone here knows Chris Hastings'. The guy who was doing the asking said, 'Could you point him out to me, please?'. The barman says, 'I haven't seen him today'. The guy, with the questions, leaves. Chris leaves his seat in the corner and walks over to the barman, Tony. He gives Tony a 50 Euro note, with a note saying, 'Thank you' in Maltese.'

'So?' said a bored looking Charlie

'Now, this Tony has a young brother, Paul, who Chris works with regularly,' continued Pup, 'Paul has a security business but he's also into tech stuff and gadgets. He repairs computers and tablets for the rich and famous, regular visitors to Malta. Many of his side hustle clients are old and don't know that much about tech stuff but they trust Paul to look after them. When his clients stop paying him or lose their influence, fall ill, die or are disgraced Paul then sells their data – copies of their disks and memory cards. That's how Chris met Paul. The moral of this story, in Chris's words, is 'As long as I keep paying enough Tony and Paul are completely trustworthy. Trust always has a price.'.

4.

Pup was loving every minute of walking around the Olympic Park with Charlie. They'd sat on the bank by the bandstand and then just meandered around taking in the party atmosphere. They'd stopped to watch a steel drums band and some highland dancers and the excited buzz with miles of smiles made the whole experience joyous and uplifting. The only annoyance was Charlie rarely looking up from the screen of her iPhone.

Pup loved the colours more than anything and remembered that Skip had said that the last great British event prior to the London

Olympics was the Isle of Wight Festival in 1970. Chris, along with six hundred thousand others, had been there and it had been Hendrix's last gig. Chris had said over forty years later he could still see the joy, peace, hope and all the colours. Pup liked the diversity, the Olympic purple and he really loved the paving of the Park with overlaying circles in pastel pink, orange, blue and yellow.

Pup and Charlie had arranged to catch up with the others in the Heineken bar area that was sponsored by Cisco. It had a big screen to watch the action, a small stage for bands, barbecue food and striped deckchairs on artificial grass. As Pup paid the entry he instinctively took hold of Charlie's hand and said, 'You're beautiful and I'm so proud to be with you'.

Charlie said 'Hell, you'd better start drinking again - you're going soft in the head'

'Nah you've made my summer and that's the first time I've ever walked among thousands looking at the woman who I'm lucky enough to be with. Give me a bit of glam celebrity any day of the week. How do all the stares and nudges make you feel?'

'Goes with the territory. I wouldn't like a massive poster of me and my bare midriff up there', pointed Charlie, 'like Victoria Pendleton. Anyway, start talking sense – there's Scalesy and Steph'.

Scalesy and Steph were sat cross legged on the artificial turf. They had their backs to the entrance, were deep in conversation and hadn't noticed Pup and Charlie. Steph was explaining to Scalesy that she thought Trude wasn't coping well since the death of her mother, Pat. 'She rarely leaves the house and avoids crowds. She won't even go to see her beloved football and cricket teams. She must be cracking up to not be here with us on the biggest day of the Olympics'.

'What's that Steph? No Trude? Good job all the world's leaders are in full attendance because the Lord Chamberlain's Men are a skeleton crew. We're reduced to just four musketeers – two are in Malta and Nick and Tricks can't make it either. It's a tragedy.'

'Trude and Nick are cracking up but what's Tricks' excuse?', said Scalesy.

'I'm not sure Scalesy – my guess is that someone in the supply chain has let him down and he needs to sort it, pronto.', said Pup, 'Anyway, Scalesy could you help me get more refreshments from the bar?'.

As soon as Pup and Scalesy were out of hearing distance from Steph and Charlie, Pup whispered 'Is Dave still working on three exploding yachts for today?'

'So, my contact tells me. I only sent plans for two. I got a message in a bottle to Chris,' said Scalesy.

'Yeah, the illusion only requires two. I got a message to him too – a postcard. It's going to be an edge of our seats day, here and in Malta.'

5.

In a back-street garage in St Julian's Bay, Malta Paul and Chris are looking at what looks like a concrete and wood builders' hut. It was made from painted polystyrene built around a wooden step ladder. In this garage, they built many floats for the festivals.

Paul was in jeans and a T shirt rather than his normal Head of Security, uniform. Paul exuded calm and confidence which is why Chris and Paul's brother, Tony, had chosen him for the job. Paul turned to Chris who was wearing an All Blacks rugby shirt with the collar up, black jeans, black trainers and a black baseball hat. 'What do you think, Boss?', Paul said.

Chris wrote on a small notebook 'Perfect'. Then he wrote 'Is my boat away from the fireworks?'. Paul nodded.

Chris wrote 'All the CCTV will be off? Paul nodded.

'Police paid and Dave's getaway car fixed?' Paul nodded and smiled.

6.

At 4.30pm in Malta on Saturday, August 4th, 2012 an immaculately uniformed Paul Grech, Head of Security for the Hilton Hotel and Yacht Club in Portamaso, walked alongside Sir Nigel Morris from the Conference Hall to the elevator.

CHAPTER TEN: The Final Solution

Cancer: One or more diseased areas consisting of new cells
growing in an uncontrolled way.

1.

'I'M BUZZING', said Pup taking his seat in the Olympic stadium. He noticed that the three spare tickets he'd sold to the touts had, in turn, been sold to three Chinese gentlemen. Charlie whispered back 'I'm worried – what if the packages I've helped deliver to the big swinging dicks here do contain explosives? What if Chris or Dave lied about my Uncle being safe in Malta?'

Pup looked at Charlie. Her usual unflappable if slightly care worn expression had a queasy edge to it that he had not seen before. She glanced at him from below haughty and impeccably plucked brows and immediately straightened her face as she saw her unease reflected in his expression.

'No worries, Charlie. He put his hand on her knee and she followed it with her eyes, tensing her muscled slightly as the hand that was meant to comfort, made touch down. All you'll hear over the coming months are that a FIFA official has grassed on Blatter to save their own neck or a bank has been ordered to compensate all its customers after another scam has come to light. If we don't know what's going to happen next you never will and whatever it is it won't be terrorism. I believe in Chris. Just enjoy.'

Steph was at the end of the row of seats, Scalesy next to her, then Charlie and Pup was next to the very excited Chinese contingent. The stadium was electric, the noise amazing, even the announcements and highlights packages on the big screen were being cheered. Nearly every one of the 75,000 spectators seemed to be waving the union jack or be wrapped in one. The expectation was gold. Below the Chamberpots to their left was the sandpit for the long jump which was close to the starting line for track events.

Scalesy: 'So we've got Greg Rutherford in the long jump. He's done great to get in the final. I'd never heard of him – had you?'

Steph: 'Me neither. Mind you the whole of Sheffield has only heard of Jess'

Steph was watching Charlie and Pup. She was an expert in picking up atmosphere and she could feel the tension that Charlie was feeling radiating out from where she and Pup were sitting. Pup had briefly and apparently ill advisedly, judging by Charlie's expression, put his hand on her knee. Charlie turned to her now and said brightly,

'That's better he ran through the first jump but he's going well now. He's got a lot of space between him and the board so he can do better still'.

Steph: 'In with a chance, hey look Jess is in the stadium for the 800'!

Pup: 'Aw the noise. My heart may not stand this'

Steph: Never mind I just hope Jess's can. Just think of the two years of pressure she's had. She always wanted to be a sprinter not a heptathlete'.

Charlie: 'Just one good run. Come on Jess'.

Pup: Go Jess

Charlie: 'Yes Jess. Stay loose'

Steph: 'She will, she will, she will'

Pup: 'J......E....S....S'

Charlie: 'Gold, gold, gold, gold'

Scalesy: 'What a smile. The most beautiful, perfect smile in the world. Jess, you little beauty'

Pup: 'Here we go again. Greg's up and Mo's about to start. Hell – this is c...r...a...z...y.'

Scalesy: 'He'll jump a world record with this noise'

Charlie: 'Looks big'

Pup: 'I'm not sure. White flag though.'

Charlie: 'Eight … thirty … one. Gold'

Pup: 'You sure?' as he hugs Charlie and they jump up and down while Scalesy and Steph swap high fives.

Steph: 'Right Mo's into it. This man will be the greatest athlete the world has seen.'

Pup: 'I'm backing Bekele'

Charlie: 'Greg has a no jump but he's got gold – listen to that noise. Why bother with seats. This is amazing'

Steph: 'Go Mo'

Charlie 'Go Mo'

Pup: 'I'm backing Mo'

Scalesy: 'It's the high-altitude training. The Kenyans and Ethiopians used to win when they came down but Mo does his training at high altitude. He's breaking them up. Once he's in front that's it'

Steph: 'Go Mo'

Charlie: 'You've destroyed them Mo'

Pup: 'Always knew it would be Mo'

Scalesy: 'See Greg with the flag over him, screaming Mo on below us'.

Steph: 'Thank you Chris. He'd have loved this.'

Scalesy: 'You little beauty – arise Sir Mo. We've been to heaven for a half hour and got ourselves three golds'

Pup: 'Y…. E… S… S' . Pup then kisses three confused Chinese gentlemen whilst singing 'All You Need Is Love', along with seventy-five thousand others.

2.

After getting back to his double bed, single occupancy, King Executive room, with Marina view, in the Hilton Hotel, Portamaso Yacht Club, Malta, Sir Nigel Morris had decided to take an afternoon power nap. He picked up the phone and put it down again. It was his alarm call. He sipped from a small bottle of fizzy water and jumped out of bed. He opened the curtains and could see the activity on the yachts and speedboats in the marina. It was still a fine, sunny afternoon. He put the television on for the Olympics coverage. He stripped off his shorts and T-shirt and naked, did a few minutes stretching exercises in front of a long mirror.

He went into the bathroom and started the shower. The lights went off. It was dark momentarily and then a spotlight fell on a small white box, which he hadn't noticed before, on the floor next to the toilet. The front of the small box opened and there emerged a large brown and red spider.

The spotlight went off. Sir Nigel fell against the door and found the handle but he couldn't open the door. Another spotlight came on. On the top of the door opening, close to the ceiling was another white, but larger, box, As Sir Nigel looked up at it, still pulling at the door handle frantically, and the box began to tip. Sir Nigel screamed. A black and yellow snake fell out. The spotlight went off.

A voice, Maltese he identified - the end of their sentences end high, like a question - reached him from a hidden speaker. The voice quietly asked, 'Would you like to come out, Sir Nigel?' The answer was in the affirmative.

Sir Nigel fell into the arms of a policeman with gun drawn and pressed immediately to Sir Nigel's temple. The policeman was wearing a Tony Blair mask. Under the mask was Paul, who thought Chris's plan was doomed because Sir Nigel was about to die from a heart attack.

Chris had, perhaps, underestimated Sir Nigel's great fear of spiders and snakes, He was perspiring, urine was running down his leg and he seemed to have forgotten how to breathe. He was biting his lip so hard it was beginning to bleed. Paul motioned to another policeman, wearing a George Bush mask to help him secure, with wire cables and locks, the quivering, Sir Nigel to a chair. There were seven cables used, from ankles to neck, and then a gag was tied and finally a quilt, from the bed thrown, over him. Paul was worried about the shivering.

Sir Nigel's, left hand, his writing hand, was free of restraint, from the elbow joint. The chair was in front of the 40' LED television,

147

which was now on high volume with a news channel on. The third policeman had already gone into the bathroom to recapture the spider and snake.

'Watch the television Sir Nigel', the picture changed to the battery of cannons below Upper Barrakka Gardens. The cannons looked as if they were pointing at a massive super yacht moored in the Grand Harbour.

'Do you know whose yacht that is, Sir Nigel? Of course, you do, you were due to meet with him later here in a private suite. There are also some very powerful people with yachts in the harbour outside too. But you knew that already.'

The super yacht in Valletta, on the television screen, appeared to suffer a massive explosion with smoke and flames obliterating the centre section of the yacht. The policeman with the George Bush mask switched off the television using the remote. The three policemen pushed the chair to the glass doors that led to the outside balcony.

'Now Sir Nigel we want you to look outside. Can you see a man in a red shirt, with a red hat? Good, now his job is to blow up yachts. Of course, not just any yachts, only the yachts of your friends at this Conference you're attending. The explosives are already in the plumbing and all Mr Red Hat must do is point and click. It's a game of chance as to whether anyone is on board – although Mr Red Hat can see who walks onto the yacht and he is instructed to blow up the yachts with people on first. Once the first yacht blows up then, of course, more people arrive on the scene, which means we get more hits with the second yacht. It's like an accumulator. There he goes, he's off to his, rather ingenious, hiding place.'

The three policemen then pushed the chair to the desk where a white laptop was open.

'Sir Nigel I'm going to explain to you the rules of our blowing up yachts, in Portamaso harbour, game. I'm going to explain them slowly and you're going to have to concentrate very hard or a lot of people, including you, are going to come to a sticky end. Is that understood?'

Sir Nigel opened his eyes wide to signal that he had understood. Paul was relieved to see this, as there was now a chance they could get the job done before Sir Nigel had his heart attack. Paul continued, loudly and slowly:

'Mr Red Hat is going to blow up a yacht, to a maximum of four, every fifteen minutes. How many yachts he blows up depends on how quickly and accurately you complete a little task. If you complete the task within fifteen minutes then no yachts explode. If it takes you over an hour then four yachts will have exploded and it is time up for you too. Do you understand Sir Nigel? You have up to an hour to complete the task but if you complete it within fifteen minutes no yachts get blown up.

Sir Nigel's eyes opened wide and so Paul could continue with the part he loved the most of his monologue, which Chris had scripted for him.

'We've come up with a little deterrent which we think should prevent you from cheating or being, in any way, slapdash in your work. We're going to leave you in the company of Incey Wincey the spider and Sheila, her of the hissy fits, the snake. They'll be in two little white boxes behind you. If you make a mistake then the little door opens to let Incey out to play. If you make two mistakes then Sheila will be out to join in the fun too. Clearly you won't be around to make a third mistake.

If you've satisfactorily completed the task then in sixty-five minutes from the start all these locks on you will automatically open. The room will remain locked down – no electricity, no doors will open, no communication is possible. We suggest that you then go straight to the bathroom and lock yourself in for fifteen minutes as the laptop and the two white boxes will destruct and we've arranged for someone to clean up the mess. We'd recommend that you then carry on with your day, meetings and conference as if nothing had ever happened. You are not the first person to have helped us with our research and so no one will ever know that you've contributed.

OK so far. Now here's how you accomplish your very simple task. The screen will show you a group of names. There will be usually between four and nine names. All the names are of people that know each other. All you must do is rank the names in terms of the power you believe they wield. So, if let's say the group was Dick Cheney, Donald Trump and Lady Gaga you'd rank Dick Cheney as One – the most powerful to get what they want in world affairs and you may guess Donald Trump two and Lady Gaga three.

Is that understood? One means the most powerful. If you don't recognise a name just put an X against the name instead of a number. We know all the names you know. We've put in some false names and we're pretty sure of the rankings so if you try to cheat we'll know and let Incey and Sheila come out to play. We'll leave you now to get on with it. The boxes are just behind you. Just follow the instructions on the screen. Here are your glasses'

Paul placed the spectacles on Sir Nigel and the three pulizijo left the room. Paul reckoned there was a 50:50 chance of Sir Nigel being well enough to complete the task but no chance at all of him cheating.

Dave was watching all this from Paul's office at RazDaz Games on the 14th floor of Portamaso Tower. He was in desperate need of a ciggy. Everything was communicated in real time from Sir Nigel's screen including pictures of Sir Nigel so Dave and others could see where he hesitated or, worst case, whether his frightened state made the task impossible so they'd need to get him out of there. Every entry Sir Nigel made was sent to the cloud and then to computers in Tripoli, Palermo, Tunis, Peking and Mumbai.

As soon as the door in the hotel room closed Dave typed out a message to appear on Sir Nigel's screen. It read:

'Good afternoon, Sir Nigel. Hope you are well. Before we start we're just going to safely explode one of our old vessels in the harbour. No-one will be hurt. This is just to take attention from the hotel to outside in the harbour. While we're doing this, please read the instructions, coming up in front of you.'

Dave trained his binoculars on Chris. Chris would ensure there were no people near the small boat moored at the furthest point nearest the sea, at Portamaso harbour. The exploding boat wasn't going to happen now though – it would happen when Sir Nigel had completed his task. The sounds of the explosion and activity in the harbour that Sir Nigel would hear now were from a micro speaker and soundtrack just below the window of the hotel room.

Chris had estimated, after many trial runs, that Sir Nigel would complete the task within eighteen to twenty-four minutes. That would mean one more fake explosion through the speakers, which Dave would orchestrate. It would therefore leave Dave at least three quarters of an hour to get to the ferry to Sicily before there was the chance of Sir Nigel's plight being discovered. It would probably be much longer because of the explosions of the concrete hut and the small boat that Dave would detonate. This diversion would ensure Sir Nigel wouldn't be a focus and there was a very good chance that Sir Nigel wouldn't say anything at all,

When Sir Nigel had completed the task, Dave would signal to Chris and Chris would signal, by standing on top of the concrete hut that there was no-one near the small boat. Dave would detonate the explosives through a timer. The timer was set for fifteen minutes after the reciprocal signals. Chris would then go inside the concrete hut to change out of his distinctive gear and leave by a newly created hole in the wall at the opposite side to the CCTV cameras.

The hut was packed with fireworks, explosives, Chris's computers, gadgets and the red canvas bag full of files. Inside the hut there were also two bottles of whisky, some sleeping pills and the two capsules that Tricks had sent him. There was also a corpse which would be wearing Chris's clothes, watch, wallet, scarf and hat. Chris had told Dave that he would get away on his boat and whenever he'd had enough of the solitude would commit suicide.

The timer that Dave had set would explode both the small boat and Chris's concrete hut. The fragments of watch, cards, Chris's red clothing, bag and unrecognisable male body parts would be enough for them to realise that their prime suspect in the case of Sir Nigel, if there was one, was no more.

It took Sir Nigel nineteen minutes to complete his tasks. Dave had arranged for explosives to be placed in Chris's get away boat. Dave and Chris reciprocated their signals. Chris went inside the hut. Instead of using the timer Dave immediately detonated the small boat, Chris's getaway boat and the concrete hut. 'Hoisted by your own petard' was the sentiment that came to Dave's mind. Dave walked into the sunshine out of the staff entrance of Portamaso Tower. He lit a cigarette and hurried across the road to the waiting car.

Dave threw his cigarette away and as his hand reached to open the car door he saw a black and gold ring pass his nose as a granite like arm raised him in the air. Dave's dead body was bundled into the car and two minutes later was carried into a concrete hut which was exploded five minutes later. There was no CCTV footage of any of these events but an eye witness did explain to a disinterested police officer that a large man in a balaclava was seen near the hut and that there was a tuft of blonde hair showing.

CHAPTER ELEVEN: Dealer Takes All

Croupier. Presides over a gaming table collecting the stakes and paying the winners.

1.

THE TIMES IN MALTA reported a 'tragic accident where a well-known foreigner, an Englishman but an enthusiast, died in a fireworks related explosion in ....' and 'very early yesterday morning in Valletta a German film crew were admonished for setting off flares from a small boat, which witnesses stated was too close to the yachts, and without the permission of the authorities. Legal proceedings may ensue....' The Independent in Malta reported that 'a small boat caught fire in Portamaso harbour yesterday. No one was hurt.'

The Independent in England and the Washington Post both reported that 'Yesterday, photographs of world leaders appeared on Facebook, without explanation. The leading politicians and business heads were from many different countries. The photographs have been removed, but the hashtags #sleaze, #corrupt and #resign have trended on Twitter as people that saw the photographs tweeted their reaction to them. One estimate suggests that as many as four hundred photographs were posted to different Facebook accounts, with more than a hundred leading figures clearly identified '

On a yacht moored in Sydney harbour, an Indian businessman had just been informed that he'd won over $194,000 on a bet. He'd bet on the time a well-known French politician would announce to the media that he was stepping down from his position, to spend more time with his family.

154

2.

On a very hot afternoon by the pool at Bar Xero on the Greek island of Kos a bald, clean shaven and well-muscled man, wearing only shorts, was talking to the barman. There were signs of sunburn on his neck. Below the sunburn, on the nape of his neck, was a small black tattoo with the masks of comedy and tragedy. Trude approached the man from behind. He hadn't seen her. Trude put one finger on the man's shoulder and said, with the hint of a laugh;

'I don't recognise that voice but I'd recognise that back anywhere. I've brought the handcuffs.'

Without turning around, the man said,

'What's Up Top Cat?'

Tony Robinson OBE is known in the UK as the Micro Business Champion and is the co-founder, with Tina Boden, of the annual #MicroBizMattersDay. He has written poetry, fiction and business books for over thirty years. The most popular of his published work is 'Freedom from Bosses Forever' which is a fictional satire. 'Freedom from Bosses Forever' is available as paperback, kindle and audio book. Tony is on a never ending (he hopes) tour with a one-hour show based on this book. Tony also has a site dedicated to all his poetry and fictional writing; FreedomfromBossesForever.com

You can follow Tony on Twitter @TonyRobinsonOBE and read more about him on Amazon and at www.TonyRobinsonOBE.com

Amanda Thomas is a writer, scriptwriter, broadcaster and journalist. Amanda has an absolute passion for creativity in whatever genre she is working in. Amanda can handle tragedy and triumph with equal sensitivity and understanding. Amanda has lived abroad and worked with all sorts of interesting people. Tony asked Amanda to help him to express the emotions of the three female characters in Loose Cannon. Like all Amanda's clients he is delighted with her work.

Lightning Source UK Ltd.
Milton Keynes UK
UKOW06f0607041117
312101UK00005B/351/P